catgirl doctor

Volume 2

By Brandon Varnell

Art by Liremi

Catgirl Doctor, Vol. 2

Brandon Varnell and Kitsune Incorporated supports the right to free expression and the value of copyright. The purpose of copyright is to encourage writers and artists to produce creative works that enrich our culture.

ISBN: 978-1-951904-16-6

dedication

This page is made in dedication to my amazing patrons. Without them, my characters would never get lewded by so many wonderful artists:

303cloud; Aaron Harris; Adam; Alarinnise; Alexander Rodriguez, Arnando Pastrana; Benjamin Collins; Benjamin Morgan; Brendan Smiley; Brennan; Bruce Johnson; Bryce McClay; C.L. Holgrahm; Catcrazy9; Chace Corso; Christopher Gross; Cody Woodard; CosmicOrange; D; Dane Smith; DeseriDan; Dhivael; Edward Lamar Stephenson; Edward P Warmouth; Emery Moore; Feitochan; Forrest Hansen; Ine Airclana; IronKing; Jacob Flores; Jacob Wojno; Jake Fedor; Jeremy Schultz; Jesus; John Patton; Kevin; Lucid Faytl Lupus Umbras; Mark Frabotta; Matthew Wallace; Max A Kramer; Michael Moneymaker; Nathan S; Omegapudding; Philip Hedgepeth; Rafael Eriksen; Raymond Tatton; Red Phoenix; Red Viking; Repooc llahsram; Richard Garret; Samuel Donaldson; Sean Gray; Seismic Wolf; Slim; Smudi Corp; Starwarscout Jon; T; Thomas Jackson; Tora Linkley; Travis Cox; Victor Patrick Bauer; William Crew; xy172; Yuriy Snyadanko; Zach Strickland; Zenn Barger

table of contents

chapter 1

It was Saturday in the afternoon when Chris and Silva found themselves inside of the Catgirl Protection Bureau Office of Catpanion and Child Registration located on Third Avenue. It was situated in between I Street and H Street. Next to the Catgirl Protection Bureau Office of Catpanion and Child Registration was a the Superior Court South Court Division and a San Diego Marriage Certificate office.

As they entered through the sliding doors, a soft jingle issued from speakers somewhere inside, alerting whoever was at the front desk that someone had arrived. The front lobby was mostly empty. There was one young couple, a human with blond hair and a catgirl with orange-striped hair. They were sitting close together and both of them had a bundle in each arm. It looked like this catgirl was one of the few who had given birth.

Chris was not sure he envied the man. Four kids sounded like a handful to him.

"Good afternoon," a woman sitting behind the front desk said to them as they entered. She had a professional smile. Her furry blonde cat ears twitched as she watched them with vivid blue eyes. "Can I help you two today?"

Chris walked hand in hand with Silva toward the front desk. His companion was looking around with curiosity, but not fear. She had gotten much better about not panicking when they went outside. He believed she might have finally gotten over her fear of being around people—for the most part.

"Yes, I'd like to register Silva as my catpanion," Chris said to the woman.

A gleam entered the woman's eyes as she nodded, placed her hands on her keyboard as though getting ready to hack into a secure database, and glanced back at him.

"Can I get the name of you and your soon-to-be catpanion?"

"My name is Chris Redford, and this is Silva…"

Chris paused when he realized that he didn't know what Silva's last name was. Whenever a catgirl was adopted into a human family, she would always take the last name of that family. However, her last guardian had been a man named Markus—Chris couldn't remember that man's last name, though he was sure Officer Demire had told him—and he was sure she didn't want to use his last name.

"Vira," Silva said at last. "See if Vira works please."

"Silva Vira." The catgirl typed into the keyboards. Chris saw the screen reflected in the woman's eyes, though he couldn't tell what it said. After a moment, she frowned, then looked at Silva with an apologetic smile. "I'm sorry... that last name doesn't appear to be registered on here."

"I guess... it was erased when Grams died... or maybe when my previous guardian took custody of me..."

When Chris saw the disheartened expression on Silva's face, the way her ears and tail drooped, he grimaced and glanced back at the receptionist.

"Is it possible to look up an older name on file?"

The receptionist bit her lips, long fangs jutting out. "It is possible, but we generally don't do that. All of our information is completely up to date. If we used the name she had from a previous guardian, it could cause legal problems."

Silva's grip on his hand tightened, but Chris did his best to maintain a calm expression. The secretary seemed to realize something was wrong. She gave them both a sincere and apologetic smile. However, she also didn't budge. Rules were rules he guessed.

"Silva?" Chris asked.

Silva made several interesting facial expressions as she struggled against her desire not to use the name of her abuser with her desire to be his catpanion. He could almost see the battle playing out in her eyes.

"Flint," she said at last. "Silva Flint."

"Silva... Su.. ci... io..." The secretary typed in Silva's new last name and more information appeared to scroll across the screen. "Ah ha! Here you are... oh..." The secretary suddenly paused as more information came up. Chris didn't know what it was, but the helpful catgirl was quick to inform them. "There's a police report attached to Ms. Flint's file. Since you're involved parties, I can tell you that it is in regards to Markus Flint and his subsequent arrest for several violations of catgirl abuse." She paused, ears flicking as her expression became more serious. "Given the nature of this situation, it should be perfectly possible to change her last name. In fact, because you, Mr. Redford, are currently listed as Silva's temporary guardian, when you sign the necessary paperwork to make her your catpanion, you can also file the papers needed to change her name."

As Silva's eyes lightened up with delight, Chris breathed a heavy sigh of relief before turning a smile on the secretary.

"Thank you for letting us know," he said.

The secretary gave him a pleased smile. "I lived with an abusive guardian once as well, so I understand not wishing to use that person's last name."

Chris was beginning to realize there were a lot more cases of catgirl abuse than he first realized. Maybe it was because he had lived a relatively sheltered life. The neighborhood he grew up in was one of the better ones, with some of the lowest crime rates in San Jose and a welcoming community well-known for its love of catgirls. It was honestly shocking when he found Elsa, unconscious and injured underneath that bridge in Memorial Park.

After thanking the secretary, Chris and Silva moved over to sit on one of the couches. Like the young couple on the other couch, they sat incredibly close together, so close that Silva might as well have been sitting on his lap. The young couple with their litter of four catgirl children smiled at them. Chris and Silva smiled back.

"Filing to make her your catpanion?" asked the man.

"That's right," Chris said.

"That's quite the step," the catgirl said. "I remember when we first filed a couple of years ago. It feels like such a long time now."

"How was it?" Silva asked, suddenly curious. When they glanced at her, she jerked reflexively as her fearful instincts kicked in but quickly mastered herself. "The process to make you his catpanion. How was it?"

"It's a relatively painless process," she said. "The only thing it requires is a bit of patience. There's a lot of paperwork that you need to fill out and sign."

"How many papers?" asked Chris, furrowing his brow.

"Not as much as filing for a loan on a house," was all the man said.

Seconds after that ominous little tidbit of information was spoken, a man came in and called for the couple. They were apparently there to get the necessary paperwork for their children filed. It was an important process and something that couldn't be done at the hospital because this was outside of their jurisdiction.

It seemed there was a lot of red tape involved with having kids.

The wait until they were called in wasn't long. A young woman with curly brown hair and kind eyes, dressed in a smart business suit, called for them. She introduced herself as Lily Sutor and led them to an office. Once there, she had them both sit down and began pulling out a large stack of papers.

"These are the papers you both need to sign," she said, then smiled when she noticed how pale their faces were as they stared at what must have been several thousand sheets of paper. "Don't worry. A lot of what's written on here is just legalese. It talks about the laws, policies, and so on involved with having a catpanion and being a catpanion. You also don't have to sign every single page. The pages where you need to sign are marked where your signatures should go."

"I-I see. That's good," Chris muttered as he grabbed the first page. A thought occurred to him and he looked up. "Can we also get the files needed to change Silva's last name?"

"It's already in there," Lily said as if she'd been expecting this question. That meant she must have looked up their file before printing these out, so she likely knew of their circumstances.

Well, whatever. That made things easier for them.

The process of signing all those documents took almost an hour. During the time when they were signing, the woman spoke to them in a matter of fact tone of voice, as if she was reciting lines she had said thousands of times already. Knowing how many catgirls became catpanions, she probably had.

"The first thing you should know is that you will be subject to the same bi-annual assessment and tests that breeders go through," Lily explained to him as he signed his name on the nth document, then slid it over to Silva so she could do the same. "We do this because, as you might have guessed already, there are quite a few serious cases of catgirl abuse. Of course, usually, we are not so sloppy in our procedures. I've read your file. After what happened, I suspect the San Diego Police Department may push for more stringent standards in regards to these evaluations."

Chris nodded to show he was listening. He'd never had to take the breeder test, but he did own a catgirl guardianship ID, which granted him the right to adopt and raise a catgirl. He had to take a test yearly to prove that he was physically and mentally fit to raise a catgirl.

"I feel like I should also tell you, Mr. Redford, that while there are no limits in how many catpanions you can have, you will have to sign a new set of documents for each one." Lily wore a smile as she explained this. "Also, depending on how many catpanions you have, you may be forced to sign even more documents and have the Catgirl Protection Bureau go through your personal records and financial history to make sure you do not have any black marks on your records and are financially secure enough to properly look after multiple catpnaions."

"I know," Chris said, then smiled. "I don't think you have to worry, though. I highly doubt I'm going to have anymore catpanions."

He glanced at Silva, expecting to see her smiling at his show of loyalty, but instead she just looked confused. There was a slight tilt to her head as she stared at him with inquisitive eyes. When he saw this, the smile on his face slowly left.

Lily gave him an amused smile. "Regardless of whether you plan to or not, I just wanted to let you know how that works in case something does happen and you find yourself with more than one catpanion."

"So I see…"

They finally finished signing all of the documents. Lily took them from him and Silva, placing them inside of a binder that she bound together with a leather chord. She informed them that the process of filing all this information could take anywhere from one week to two months depending on how backed up they were. At the moment, it seemed the process would be fairly quick as there were not many new people presently filing to become catpanions.

As they left the Catgirl Protection Bureau Office of Catpanion and Child Registration, Chris and Silva paused just outside the door as the fresh air hit them. It was a bit chilly, but the air was getting a tad warmer. At least, he thought so. The afternoon sky hung high overhead. He looked at the sun as a gentle breeze blew across the street.

"Shall we head home?" asked Chris.

"Yes." Silva nodded. "There's a new episode of *Masterchef Junior* on tonight that I want to see."

"We can't miss that," Chris said.

Truth be told, while he didn't mind watching Gordon Ramsay's cooking shows, for the most part, he wasn't too keen on the junior one. It was a blow to his pride. That might have sounded like a joke if he said it out loud, but the truth was it hurt his pride to watch kids not even half his age outcook him.

While he never considered himself a great chef since he only knew how to create simple dishes and follow directions, he still liked to think he was a better cook than most adult men. His own dad had no cooking talent whatsoever. About the only thing his dad could make was grilled cheese sandwiches and spaghetti. Even then, he didn't create his own homemade sauce but used Prego bought by the jar.

His mom did all the cooking at home.

As they walked toward the bus stop across the street, Chris wondered what his life would have been like if he had decided to become a chef. He glanced at Silva as they walked toward the bus stop.

It didn't sound as exciting as his current life.

***

That evening, Chris made a simple dinner of tuna garlic pasta. It was easy to make. He simply boiled a salted pot of water for the pasta and cooked it according to the directions.

He'd used a wheat pasta instead of normal pasta. Once the pasta was close to being ready, he added some oil to a small pan and cooked garlic over medium heat for about 30 seconds before adding in the tuna, lemon juice, and parsley. The meal only took about fifteen minutes to create, and he had added Parmesan cheese, lemon zest, and some salt and pepper for seasoning.

Silva had loved it.

"I think you should really consider being on Chef Gordon's TV show," Silva said as she sat with her head in his lap. Her warm cheek rested against his thigh. It was a pleasant feeling.

Chris shook his head. "My cooking is nowhere near the level expected of people who go on Chef Gordon's show. All of those people are professional chefs who own or work at restaurants and have spent their entire lives cooking."

"The kids aren't professionals."

"The kids are too young to be professionals, and even if they aren't, their cooking is already better than mine."

As they spoke, Chris ran his fingers through Silva's hair and rubbed her ears. A low purring sound emitted from the back of Silva's throat. When he looked down, it was to find her small mouth parted as she took slow and deep breaths. The pinkness of her cheeks complimented her porcelain skin as she rubbed her face against him.

Chris grew hard.

"You're poking me," Silva said.

"You're rubbing your face against me," Chris countered. "And you're doing it on purpose."

"Mmm… maybe I am."

While Silva was often shy and didn't like being around people, she didn't have as much trouble asserting her desires to him—at least, not anymore. She used to, but after he helped her get over the survivors guilt she'd been suffering from and asked her to become his catpanion, she had become a lot more forthright toward him.

"Your scent is so thick," Silva murmured as she nuzzled her nose against his crotch. Chris's breathing picked up as his cock twitched in his pants.

"Is… that a good thing?" he asked.

"I like your scent, so I think it is."

As she spoke, Silva climbed off the couch and knelt on the floor. She reached out with her teeth, grabbed his zipper, and pulled it down. Meanwhile, she unbuttoned his pants, then grabbed the hem of his jeans, and slid them down his hips. To help her, Chris lifted his hips off the couch, allowing her to slide them off until they were around his ankles.

With his pants no longer confining him, Chris's dick sprang up, creating a pitch tent out of his boxer shorts. Silva licked her lips as reached out and removed his boxers next. As his dick emerged, fully erect and throbbing, Silva's breathing picked up. Her catlike pupils seemed to dilate as she stared at his penis.

At the moment, Silva was wearing simple pajamas. Her shirt was several sizes too large and had a large hole for her head. Because it was so big, one side was sliding down her left shoulder, revealing a good amount of bare skin and collarbone. As she leaned over, Chris caught a glimpse of her small breasts,

Then Silva was leaning all the way forward, holding his dick with one hand as she rubbed her cheek along the shaft. An electric jolt raced through him. It was an affectionate gesture similar to when a cat rubbed against its owner's leg... except this held an eroticism no cat could ever possess. Watching this cute girl as she nuzzled his cock was easily one of the hottest things he'd ever seen.

"It's so warm," she breathed. "And it always twitches in my hand."

"T-that's because your hands are cold," Chris tried to explain, but it was hard when Silva's soft fingers and cheek were rubbing against his dick.

"Does that mean I should warm it up?" Silva looked up at him with bright eyes that seemed innocent and pure. It made an incredible contrast to what she was doing. "My mouth is pretty warm. I read on the internet that men like it when a woman sucks them off."

"You've been reading some strange articles," Chris murmured, but that was about all he could say because Silva had just sucked the mushroom-shaped head of his cock into her mouth. He gritted his teeth and tried not to blow his load as she swirled her tongue around his head, flicking it over his piss slit. Her tongue was tiny and cute, but it had a rough texture similar to a cat's tongue. He guessed this was another one of those differences between humans and catgirls. "Oh... oh, God..."

A few seconds after she had sucked in his head, Silva moved her head down. She only managed to fit about a quarter of his dick into her mouth. When she tried going further, she coughed and sputtered as she jerked her head back.

"D-don't try to take in more than you can fit," Chris said.

Silva frowned as she leaned back, removing his now glistening cock from her mouth with a wet *plop*. The cool night air made goosebumps appear on his skin, now drenched in her saliva. She pouted up at him.

"But I heard it's better if I deep throat you."

"Girl, what articles are you reading while I'm at college?"

"What do you mean?" Silva tilted her head. "I'm reading articles that will help me be a better catpanion."

He had no idea what sort of websites she had gone to for knowledge, but he was pretty sure they were mostly sites that dealt with the purely sexual aspect of a relationship. Of course, sex was often considered the be all end all of relationships, the most important aspect—if you read articles in Magazines. He couldn't go to a grocery store without seeing at least six magazines with a "how to spice up your sex life" title on the front cover.

Come to think of it, Silva had also been reading some of those whenever they went shopping.

Before Chris could reflect more on this, Silva decided to try a different approach, and he gasped out loud and threw his head back when she took her small tongue to the underside of his cock. The sensation of a rough but tiny tongue traveling from his balls all the way to the tip of his dick blew him away. It was far different from any blowjobs he'd been given before. Pleasure raced through his body like an electric current. That tongue should have been classified as a man slayer.

After lathering his dick in saliva, Silva reached up and began pumping his shaft with her hands. At the same time, she leaned down and took what she was able to fit inside of her tiny mouth and swirled her tongue around it. Before he knew what he was doing, Chris was massaging Silva's hair as if goading her on. However, he came to quickly and realized he would cum if she kept this up.

"H-hold on! Stop!"

Silva did stop, and while she didn't remove his dick from her mouth, she did glance up at him. Chris almost shuddered. Seeing this girl with her wide and innocent eyes as she shoved his dick in her mouth was one of the most awe-inspiring sights he'd ever seen. Combined with the feel of her wet and warm mouth wrapped around him, and he was almost ready to cum right there.

"If you... keep that up... I'll cum and we won't be able to have sex."

Silva removed his dick from her mouth, a suitably horrified expression on her face. "That would be bad."

"Right. It would be." Chris smiled at her. "Come back up here, Silva. And remove your pants please."

Silva did as she was told, standing up and sliding both her pink pajama bottoms and cotton panties down her hips. When Chris caught a glimpse of her bare pussy, a deep longing to push his tongue into her folds and explore her body made his cock throb even more. It swelled in size, especially when he noticed how her pussy was glistening slightly with arousal. He wanted to taste her so badly.

But he held himself back.

"Come here."

He reached out with both hands, palms pointed up, and Silva gave him a wide smile as she placed her hands in his and allowed Chris to pull her in. She sat with her legs on either side of him, straddling his body. His dick was trapped between them, resting against her stomach, pulsating like a beating heart.

Before he buried his dick inside of her, Chris leaned forward and pressed their lips together. During their kiss, Silva wrapped her arms around his neck and pulled him close as if seeking to consume him, like she was trying to suck out his soul through his mouth. While she didn't suck out his soul, she did end up with her mouth full of his tongue.

"Hhrrrrn!!! Hrn! Hrn!"

A loud noise that was somewhere between a moan and a purr escaped Silva's mouth. It was such an erotic sound that Chris could not help but long to hear it again. That was why he reached out, slipped his hands underneath her shirt, and placed them over her chest.

Silva's chest was small. He remembered shopping with her for bras once she filled out thanks to the dietary supplements she'd been taking, and her bra size was a 38A. He didn't know exactly what a 38A bra size entailed, but suffice it to say, she had small boobs. At most, they were a little less than a handful.

However, they were very, *very* sensitive.

"Mreow!"

Silva released a low mewling sound, then squeaked when his fingers found her nipples. She didn't stop kissing him, but as he massaged her chest and swirled his fingers around her nipples, the sounds she produced were like music to his ears. Her body shuddered and rocked back and forth against him, as if seeking more pleasure through grinding her pussy on his leg. He drew his index finger in a circle around her left nipple, then flicked it back and forth. Her nipple was already hard. It protruded like a tiny button from her chest.

"Shirt off," he said.

Silva removed her hands from around his neck and raised them so he could pull her shirt off. He tossed it to the side. Now her entire body was exposed. Her snow white skin made her look incredibly fragile, like an expensive china doll that would shatter if dropped. Her skin contained a beautiful and healthy glow. Meanwhile, the soft swells of her breasts were capped with very light pink nipples that went exceedingly well with her skin tone.

Since she was now naked, Chris removed his own shirt, threw it on the coffee table behind Silva, and leaned forward. He placed his hands on the small of her back, drew her close, and pressed his mouth against her left nipple. As he sucked it into his mouth, Silva released another one of those wonderful meows. Her hands went into his hair as he flicked her nipple with his tongue. The salty taste of her skin and the light floral scent of her soap aroused him so much he was surprised he could still think straight.

"Chris! Chris! That—meow! Keep doing that! Just like that! Mreow! Please!"

Silva's nipples were so sensitive it was actually possible to bring her to orgasm just by playing with them. He wasn't sure if that was something unique to her species of catgirl or just her, but he'd made her cum several times merely from sucking on her tits. However, he didn't just suck on her breasts. When her body began glistening with a light layer of sweat, he removed his mouth from her nipple and licked the center of her chest.

"NYA!"

Silva buried her face into his hair as he did this. Her hips jerked forward as she ground her pelvis against his hard cock. The sensation of her sodden pussy lips rubbing him without his dick sliding into her warm cunt sent electric shockwaves through his body. A mind-numbing pleasure caused his vision to turn hazy, as if everything was being cast in a layer of red.

Finally, neither of them could take it anymore.

"Inside," Silva moaned. "I need it... inside! Meow!"

He was positive she had been trying to say "now." In either event, Chris didn't want to hold out anymore either. He grabbed her hips, helped her line up with his dick, and then slowly pushed her down.

"Nnnggg!!!"

A low groan escaped their lips as Chris found his cock buried inside of her. She was so incredibly tight that just moving was a chore, though that chore also brought indescribable pleasure. Her vice-like walls sucked in his dick and kept it there as if seeking to embrace him. He felt the way her walls pulsed around his cock. The erratic twitching was a sensation that couldn't be described with words alone.

"You're always... so tight," Chris grunted.

"You're always so big," Silva returned fire. "I feel... so stuffed. I think your dick is touching my womb."

"Is it really? You're okay, right?"

Silva nodded as she gazed up at him with a smile, eyes half-lidded and pleased. She reached out and cupped his cheeks, a gesture he normally did to her, but she'd been doing this more often lately.

"I love this feeling. I've never... felt this way before. I feel fulfilled. I know that sounds weird, but one of the times where I'm most satisfied is when you're inside of me."

Well, if that wasn't the most ego-boosting thing anyone had ever said to him, he didn't know what was. Those words alone were enough to make his cock swell even more. Silva's eyes widened when she felt this.

"You can get bigger?!"

"Seems that way."

Chris couldn't keep himself contained anymore and thrust his hips up. Silva released a loud cry as she arched her back. However, she kept her arms around his neck so she wouldn't fall off the couch. Chris moved back down, feeling the ridges of her pussy rub against him in the most delicious ways. It was enough to make him delirious.

He thrust his hips again. Silva cried out some more. The sound of her mewling spurned him on.

It did not take long for them to work out a pace. The sound of their hips rhythmically slapping together echoed around them and mixed with their moans, groans, grunts, and meows. As he kept his hands on her hips, he watched as her breasts bounced up and down. They didn't bounce too much since they were so small, but the slight jiggle motions enticed him. He couldn't suck her nipples into his mouth, but he did lean in and began licking her.

"MREOW! Meow! Mreeeeooooowww!"

Silva opened her mouth in a wide "O" shape before she clenched her teeth. Drool leaked down from her lips as she began panting, ragged noises now mixing in. Her hips continued to move, up and down, as his dick slid in and out of her pussy, stretching her lips wide. The way her stomach muscles flexed like a belly dancer as she moved brought a

new kind of eroticism to the table. Chris wished he could have taken a moment to lick her stomach.

Chris grunted as he tried to keep himself from cumming, tried to resist the way his balls tightened. He wanted Silva to orgasm first. If nothing else, he prided himself on putting her pleasure before his own.

Fortunately, Silva's entire body went completely rigid seconds before he shot his load inside of her. Her muscles stiffened as she hugged his head to her chest and released a loud "MREOOOOWW!" that he was sure the neighbors could hear. The juices of her pussy flowed around his cock and stained his legs. Seconds after she came, Silva's arms went slack as she slid down and slumped against his chest.

Chris sighed as he placed his hands on Silva's sweaty back and stroked her spine. Silva shivered as a soft purring noise reached his ears.

"I love…" Silva mumbled.

"Hmm?"

"I love having sex."

Chris chuckled. "Me too."

***

After they recovered enough to walk, Chris and Silva took a quick shower before heading to bed. They didn't bother wearing pajamas and simply slept naked. Silva preferred it that way, saying she liked feeling his skin against hers. She told him it was comforting.

However, as they slept, Chris was woken up by a loud ringing sound.

"Meow?!"

Silva was too.

As they sat up in bed, Silva twisting her head all over the place to try and locate the source of the noise with a panicked look in her sleepy eyes, Chris stumbled out of bed and made his way to the desk. His phone was lit up and vibrating. It was also the source of the ringing. He glanced at the caller ID on the screen and frowned when he realized it was the San Diego Police Department.

"Hello?" he said after accepting the call.

"Hello. Is this Chris Redford?" a familiar voice on the other end said.

"Officer Demire? Is something wrong?"

Chris recognized the voice as the redhead from the San Diego Police Department's Catgirl Protection Bureau branch. He felt a bit irritable as he wondered why she was calling, but he tried not to let her hear it in his voice.

"I'm sorry for calling so late... or early, I guess. I just wanted to let you know that the catgirls who were abused by Markus Flint have been relocated after getting their

checkups. They are residing at the Chula Vista Christian Orphanage for Abandoned Catgirls. It's traditionally not one we would use, but the top brass apparently decided to temporarily have them stay there for some reason. The one Silva called Kuro is also residing there."

Chris had never heard of the Chula Vista Christian Orphanage for Abandoned Catgirls before, but he found it a bit odd that the catgirls weren't being relocated to a catgirl shelter or one of the catgirl only housing units. That said, there were far more important things to consider right now.

He suddenly forgot about how she'd contacted him late at night. His throat felt a little parched as a strange sense of relief washed through him. He didn't know these girls, but he knew they were important to Silva, and that was all that mattered to him.

"I understand. Thank you for letting me know."

"You're welcome."

As Officer Demire hang up, Chris placed the smartphone on his desk and turned to Silva. Her head was tilted in that adorable manner she made whenever she was curious about something. The blanket was currently pooled around her waist, so her breasts were on display. Her cute little nipples were a bit puffy and goosebumps had appeared on her skin. While it was an attractive sight, he wasn't really in the mood to get frisky again.

"That was Officer Demire," he said to her unspoken question. "She's found Kuro and the others."

Silva's eyes widened. "Then...?"

"We can go see them tomorrow... um... later today."

As Silva sniffled, just barely containing her tears of happiness, Chris scratched the back of his head. It looked like tomorrow... um, today would be another busy day. He glanced at the clock and grimaced. It was still 2:30AM. He hoped they would be able to get a few more hours of sleep before they left to visit the orphanage.

chapter 2

Waking up with a naked catgirl at his side and something soft and delicate wrapped around his cock made Chris go from "just barely conscious" to "wide awake" in seconds. He glanced at his side. Silva was still asleep. However, there was a wide smile on her face and she seemed pleased by something. When he pulled up the covers and glanced down, he realized that what had wrapped around his dick was her soft tail.

Now that he was in this situation, Chris wondered what a tail job would feel like…

He shook his head. Now wasn't the time for that.

Unwrapping Silva's tail from around his dick—and hoping his erection would settle down because he so did not need to have a case of blue balls—Chris climbed out of bed, careful not to disturb Silva, and wandered over to his desk. He checked the time on his smartphone and saw that it was 7:00am. That was relatively early for a Sunday. He didn't need to wake up for awhile yet.

Chris crawled back into bed. Silva, as if sensing his sudden return, scooted over and draped herself across him like an extra set of sheets—a very cute extra set of sheets. She murmured something in herself, then affectionately rubbed her nose against his shoulder. That was fine and all, but then she slid her leg up his shaft and Chris suddenly had a lot more to worry about.

With a sigh, Chris realized he wasn't going to get any sleep while Silva was rubbing him like this. He thought about waking her, but she looked so cute while she was sleeping that he didn't have the heart. That being the case, he climbed back out of bed, sat down at his desk, and turned on his computer.

He might as well work on commissions while he waited for the time to whittle down.

As he opened his spreadsheet, Chris looked at the commissions currently waiting for him. He had six. One of them was from a man who had commissioned him to draw his catpanion in an anime-style of artwork. He already had the lineart for that finished. It was the man's catpanion dressed in a racey two-piece bikini and lying on the beach in a sexy pose. After thinking for a moment, he opened that one in photoshop and got to work.

Time passed by as Chris worked on his art commission. Sometime during his work, a yawn that sounded a lot like a slow "meeeeooooowwww..." echoed out from behind him, letting Chris know Silva had woken up. There was some rustling of sheets, followed by a soft thump as her feet in the floor. Moments later, Silva was peering over his shoulder with sleepy eyes.

"Is this one of those commissions you do?" she asked.

"That's right." Chris didn't take his eyes off his work, even as Silva placed her chin on his shoulder and watched him."I can't remember when I started exactly, but when I was younger, I used to really love drawing. I guess it's because I watched a lot of anime and stuff back then—"

"You still do," Silva said, though he could tell from the tone in her voice that she didn't mean anything malicious by it.

"—and at some point, I began posting my work online," Chris continued without missing a beat. "Some people eventually began encouraging me to draw more. I eventually began getting art requests, which I did at first, but then another artist I talked to back then asked why I was doing requests and not charging people. It got me thinking... I'll never be a professional artist because I don't have the gumption for it, but if I could make a quick buck or two by drawing some dude's lady in a skimpy thong, it wouldn't be a bad way to earn a bit of extra spending money."

"Meow..." Silva pushed herself against him further. She nuzzled her cheek against his. It was a very catlike action. "I don't know much about any of that, but I can tell you're a good artist."

"Thanks."

Chris continue working with Silva watching on, and by the time he finished the artwork, it was already 9:00am, which meant they needed to get a start on their day.

He shut off his computer. Together with Silva, he went toward his drawer and began pulling out clothes. While he dressed in simple pants and a black shirt with a young man who had black hair with a silver fringe on the front, Silva donned a pair of short jean shorts, white stockings, and a long-sleeved shirt that had a split in the shoulders. Her cat tail was sticking out of the tail hole, waving back and forth like a pendulum.

Chris only made a simple breakfast of scrambled eggs seasoned with salt, pepper, and shredded cheddar. He wasn't interested in making anything complicated. And Silva didn't complain. She ate it with the same gusto she ate all his food.

However, as they sat at the living room table, she asked him an odd question.

"Do you think you can teach me how to cook?"

"You want to learn how to cook?" Chris tilted his head, his fork full of eggs halfway to his mouth.

Silva nodded as she stirred her eggs around with her fork. "I've been thinking a lot, and I realized that all I really do right now is sit at home and wait for you to come back. I haven't really done anything to contribute to this household." Chris opened his mouth, but she kept talking. "I know you said I didn't have to do anything to repay you, but that's not what this is. I just want to be helpful. I want to be useful to you... you know?"

Chris closed his mouth and thought over her words, then nodded. "I understand. In that case, I'll start teaching you how to cook."

"Thank you!" Silva said with a bright smile.

Chris smiled at her in return.

The Chula Vista Christian Orphanage for Abandoned Catgirls was, as the somewhat long name suggested, located next to a church. Located in one of the less fortunate parts of Chula Vista, the church and the orphanage attached to it looked dilapidated. The shingles of the roof were worn and cracked in some places, the walls were faded, and weeds had overgrown the front lawn.

Chris had not been to church in years. His parents weren't the religious sort. Back when he was younger and they lived with his grandfather, they had attended church every Thursday and Sunday like a normal Christian family, but they stopped going after his grandfather died. He didn't even know if his parents were religious or had just been humoring his grandfather.

While churches and religion were still a big thing, less and less people were going to them as things like work and earning enough money to pay bills took precedence. Lots of people lived in the now and didn't really think about what would happen after death. Most people were skeptics like Chris anyway and didn't believe in life after death. Once you were dead, it was all over.

"Is this it?" Silva asked.

"This is where Officer Demire said they are," Chris said, shrugging.

Silva gazed at the building with an unfathomable look as her ears twitched and her tail curled around itself. Whether she thought this place was too shabby to be an orphanage or not, he could definitely tell this place housed catgirl orphans. There were a couple of catgirls playing just outside of the building. Someone had drawn squares into the sidewalk and it looked like they were playing hopscotch.

Man, that really brought him back. He never would have suspected kids still played that game.

"Come on."

Chris grabbed Silva's hand and led her toward the door. The catgirls playing hopscotch all looked at him and Silva, eyes widening in surprise, but they bolted when he got closer. That... kinda hurt actually. He hoped they didn't think he was a scary monster or anything.

They reached the front door and entered, traveling into a somewhat dingy hallway. The kids who had run in before them weren't around, but Chris heard voices off to the side, past a door on his left. It sounded like the kids were shouting for someone.

"Sister Ann! Sister Ann! A strange man and a catgirl have come!"

"He looks scary!"

"The man is all big and has muscles!"

As he listened to the kids talk, Chris felt a slight ache in his chest as he turned to Silva.

"Am I really that scary?"

"I don't think you're scary at all," Silva said, smiling brightly. "And I like your muscles, so don't worry."

Chris nodded but still didn't feel much better. However, at that moment, a woman emerged from the doorway. She was dressed in a nun's habit, the standard black and white outfit with a cross on the front. Her headdress concealed her hair, though a few strands of blonde still poked out. She had blue eyes and looked a lot younger than Chris would have expected from a nun.

"Can I help you two?" she asked as the catgirls hid behind her.

"Um…" Silva started, then stopped.

Chris saw this and spoke up next. "I received a call from Officer Demire of the San Diego Police Department's Catgirl Protection Bureau this morning. She said several victims of catgirl abuse were relocated here." Chris gestured toward the silver-haired catgirl next to him. "Silva was also a victim of the same man, so she wanted to see the catgirls and reconnect with them."

"Oh, I see." The woman's eyes widened before she clasped her hands and smiled. "Yes, I understand. We did have six catgirls move in just the other day." She paused before her smile turned a tad brittle. "They have been through quite a lot, so they are currently recuperating, but I can take you to see them."

"We appreciate that," Chris said.

"T-thank you very much!" Silva added.

Sister Ann, who Chris learned her full name was Annabelle Grace, lead them through the hallway and into a larger room. It looked like this place was a playroom. There were quite a few kids playing around, though a lot of them stopped when Chris and Silva entered alongside Sister Ann. It wasn't just catgirls who were playing there like Chris expected. There were also a couple of humans.

"You don't just accept catgirls?" Chris asked.

"We are not an officially recognized catgirl orphanage," Sister Ann explained. "The Church welcomes everyone, and so do we. Because of our policy to accept anyone who has been abandoned, the state won't recognize us as an official catgirl orphanage despite our name."

That would explain why this place looked so shabby. If they had been a state recognized catgirl orphanage, they would have been given funds to properly rebuild this dilapidated building. This did make him wonder why the abused catgirls had been moved to this particular orphanage over one that was officially recognized, but he didn't think asking a question like that would be appropriate.

"Most of the catgirls are in here," Sister Ann said as she gestured toward the door. She glanced at Chris. "Um, I hate to ask this of you, but could you remain outside? I do not know if they would take well to a man entering the room. Quite a few of them are very... skittish, even around the children."

"I understand." Nodding, Chris looked at Silva. "Will you be fine on your own?"

"Yes, I'll be fine." Silva smiled at Chris before squeezing his hand as if to reassure him.

When Silva went inside the room, Chris cocked his head to the side and listened. Seconds after the door closed, cries of "SILVA!" went up before a rushing of footsteps and a horde of voices echoed from the other side. He smiled when Silva's distinct "Mreow!" of surprise also echoed from inside the room.

"That girl seems very well-adjusted," Sister Ann said. The smile she turned on Chris was warm and gentle, like a soft summer breeze. "You must be an awfully incredible young man. I can tell she loves you a lot."

"Thank you." Chris accepted her praise with a calm smile, though he did feel a bit like blushing. Coughing into his hand, he looked at the sister again and asked, "Since it looks like I might be here for awhile, is there anything I can do to help out? I'd be bored to death if I was just sitting here."

"We are preparing lunch," Sister Ann said with a wide smile. "Do you think you can help set the tables?"

"I'll get right on that," Chris said.

It looked like this orphanage had a room that vaguely resembled a cafeteria. It was just a large room with several long tables. The tables looked old and weren't what he would have called stable. Standard metal tables that all had different lengths and sizes with a mishmash of differently shaped plastic chairs. There was no uniformity among anything. Chris suspected everything they possessed had been donated to them.

Sister Ann continued leading Chris through the cafeteria toward a door on the other side, which turned out to be a small kitchen. The moment they entered, a strong but fragrant scent hit his nose, causing Chris to take several whiffs. It smelled like someone was creating a type of soup or stew with tomatoes as the base. He glanced around the room, then stopped when he saw the person standing in front of a large pot.

The person stirring a ladle in the pot looked like a delinquent with slick-backed hair, narrowed and vicious eyes, and a somewhat slouched posture. While seeing a delinquent wearing an apron and cooking was indeed shocking, what shocked Chris more was that he knew this person.

"It's you!" he shouted.

"Huh?" The delinquent, a young man known as Jason Barker, turned his head to look over at him. When he saw who was standing in the doorway with Sister Ann, his eyes bulged from their sockets as he dropped the ladle into the pot and stumbled backward. "What the hell are you doing here?!"

"Oh, do you two know each other?" asked Sister Ann when she saw how Chris and Jason stared at each other.

"You could say that," Chris replied.

"Che!" Jason just spat to the side.

"What have I told you about spitting indoors?" Sister Ann chided Jason with a smile, which actually caused the young man to flinch. Now there was an interesting reaction. Chris wondered about the relationship between these two. He didn't ask because it wasn't any of his business, but he couldn't deny he was curious.

Sister Ann was the one who informed Jason about what Chris was doing here. Chris let her do as she pleased and asked her where the plates and utensils were, then went about grabbing everything and setting up the tableware in the cafeteria.

According to the sister, each orphan had their own assigned seating and plate. The name for each person was located on the bottom of the plate, letting him know which plate belonged to who. Under her guidance, he set the plates on the tables according to the seating arrangements.

The catgirls who had come from the hospital were all seated away from the main group. As Chris placed their plates and utensils on the table, he wondered if their seating arrangement had been made for their sake or because there were no more seats available anywhere else.

While he set the tables, Jason finished making lunch and brought the large pot of stew into the cafeteria. He set the massive thing on a table in the back. As he did that, a soft chime rang throughout the building, which alerted the kids that lunch was ready. It wasn't long before the hurried footsteps of several dozen children began echoing to him from the hallway. This was, of course, seconds before the door burst open and a horde of kids entered the cafeteria.

Chris stood near the corner as the kids moved in a surprisingly orderly fashion. They grabbed their plates, lined up in front of the table with the pot of stew, and waited for Jason to serve them.

As the kids all lined up, a group of catgirls also walked into the room, though they did not rush over to the table like the children. These catgirls were older than everyone else. Their ages appeared to vary. Some looked to be about Silva's age (Chris had discovered through her files that Silva was 19 years old), but others seemed to be in their late twenties or early thirties. Among them, Chris spotted Silva and another woman right next to her.

The woman standing next to Silva was big. Chris didn't mean that she was overweight, however. Taller than him by at least two or three heads, the woman's body muscular arms were visible thanks to the sleeveless shirt she wore. Her arms were not bulky, but she had incredible muscle definition. Her biceps and triceps flexed as she moved her arms. She looked like she could crush his head like a grape if she wanted to.

Not only did she have powerful-looking arms, but her chest was impressive. Chris didn't know what bra size she was, but her sleeveless shirt stretched across her massive bust as if it could barely contain her breasts. This also had the effect of making the shirt rise up to reveal her toned stomach. The woman had a six-pack. Very impressive.

Aside from her massive breasts and impressive physique, her incredibly dark complexion stood out to Chris. Her dark skin complimented her curly dark hair, which looked like the wild mane of a lion. Her black tail, which jutted out from a pair of carpenter pants, was longer and had a panther-like feel. Yes, it kind of reminded him of a jungle predator.

The only other thing of note was that her left arm was in a sling.

"Ah! Chris!"

Silva noticed him and grabbed the tall woman by the hand, leading her over to where he was standing. As they walked, the panther catgirl eyed him with her sharp green eyes, which contained the same vibrant glow as most predatory felines.

He smiled at Silva. "You look happy. Was it nice seeing the other catgirls?"

"It was!" Silva confirmed with a bright smile. She looked far more at peace with herself than he'd ever seen her. Pulling the other catgirl, though it looked more like the other catgirl was *allowing* Silva to pull her along, she gestured with her right hand and introduced the woman. "This is Kuro! She's the one who attacked Markus and let me escape."

"It's nice to meet you," Chris said with a respectful nod as he held out his hand. "I'm Chris."

The woman frowned as she reached out and gripped his hand. Her grip was like steel. He didn't know if she was doing it on purpose, but it felt like she was trying to crush the bones in his hand.

"My name is Kuro," the woman said. Her voice was deep and husky, the kind of voice that a lot of men would love to hear calling their name. At the same time, there was a steel-like hardness in her voice that was difficult to ignore. "Silva has said a lot about you already. It seems you've been taking *really* good care of her." There was something about the way that she emphasized "really good care of her" that made Chris wonder what Silva had told the others. "Thank you for looking after her. I greatly appreciate it."

"It's no trouble," Chris said with a shake of his head. "Silva is important to me, but even if she wasn't, I couldn't leave someone in her situation without doing everything I could to help."

"You do seem like a good guy. I hope you'll keep taking care of Silva," Kuro said as she released her grip on his hand.

"Of course," Chris said. He wanted to shake his hand out, but he thought that would make him seem weak, so he just smiled at the woman.

After all the kids had been given their meal, the older catgirls went up and were served. When this happened, Sister Ann served them instead of Jason, who they all seemed to fear... not that he could blame them. He might be a tsundere, but Jason did have that delinquent appearance and looked like the kinda guy who would rough you up if you so much as looked at him wrong.

Chris let Silva spend time with the other catgirls who'd been under Markus's tender mercies and sat with Jason. The man did not look pleased to find him sitting at the same table, but he didn't say anything either.

"I never expected to find you taking care of orphans," Chris admitted as he ate from the small bowl of stew he'd been served. It was indeed a tomato stew with vegetables and chicken inside.

"If I had my way, no one would have ever found out about this," Jason muttered.

"Is it that bad if people discover you watch over orphans?" asked Chris.

"Maybe you don't know how things work around here, but this part of Chula Vista isn't what I'd call safe," Jason informed him. "A lot of people here are poor and the crime rate in this area is pretty high. Being someone who was born and raised in this part of town, I have a reputation to uphold. If people knew I was looking after kids in my free time, that reputation would take a hit, and some idiots might get funny ideas and try to start something with me."

Maybe it was because Chris grew up in a fairly good neighborhood with nearly zero crime, but he couldn't understand where Jason was coming from. However, his words reminded Chris of this movie he saw once. It was about gangsters living in New York. What was it called again? He couldn't remember the name. It had been a long time since he'd watched it.

"I don't think you have to worry about that," Chris said. "I don't plan to say anything to anyone."

"Good."

Conversation stopped after that. Chris ate the bland stew, which hadn't been seasoned properly. He sighed. It had smelled so good when it was being made, but he guessed that was just thanks to scent of the tomatoes as they were being stewed.

As lunch continued, Chris looked at all the kids as they ate and chatted with each other. Despite how little they had, no one complained and everyone was smiling. He wondered if they didn't complain because they didn't know how little they had, but Chris knew his line of thinking came from a privileged position. It was hard for him to understand the simple joy they felt at being fed and having a roof over their heads because he'd never had to struggle to survive.

His thoughts were interrupted when the door to the cafeteria suddenly opened with a bang. He and everyone else looked in that direction as several people walked through the now open door.

The man in the lead had the kind of slimy appearance Chris expected from a greedy car salesman. He wore a tacky business suit and carried a briefcase. There was a smug and arrogant smile plastered on his face that Chris found himself wishing he could wipe off… with his fist. Yeah, Chris wanted to punch this guy's lights out after just a single glance. Behind the man were two burly dudes in similarly tacky suits, but unlike the guy in front, they were clearly bodyguards. Both of them were big and bulky, with buzzed heads and sunglasses. They looked like bouncer stereotypes.

As the man walked in, Chris wondered what the heck was going on, and what the heck was up with those suits.

"Sister Ann," the man in front greeted. Chris grimaced. Even his voice and smiled were slimy. "It looks like you are doing well. I'm sure you know why I've come."

Chris looked at Sister Ann, whose hands had clenched into fists. Her arms were trembling and her face had been drawn taut, like a bowstring pulled so far back it was about to snap. He glanced from her to Jason. The young man was clenching his fists so hard his knuckles had turned white. There was an indescribable look of hatred on his face, but he didn't open his mouth at all, and was instead biting his lip.

"I know why you've come," Sister Ann said at last. "Let's not discuss this here. We can talk in my office."

"Good. Good. Lead the way, dear sister."

Sister Ann walked past the three men and left the cafeteria. The man in the lead chuckled and followed her out of the room, his two thugs trailing after him. As the door closed behind them, everyone expelled a deep breath as if they'd just now realized they were holding their breath.

"Who was that?" Chris asked Jason.

"That was Calvin Lafaard," Jason answered, slowly unclenching his fists. "He's sort of like a small-time crime boss in this area. He came to Sister Ann when she was struggling to keep this place afloat and offered her a loan. Because she wasn't able to get a loan from the bank and donations haven't been enough to keep this place from going under, she had no choice but to accept his offer. However, his interest rates are too high for her to afford and there were numerous hidden fees in the contract that she didn't know about when signing."

"So he's a loan shark," Chris said with a frown.

Chris didn't know much about loan sharks. To be honest, he thought they were fictional characters found in anime, those guys in the suits with the slicked back bleached hair who looked like Yakuza. Actually, that dude in the middle, that Calvin guy, had looked a bit like a Yakuza... if Yakuza were American and not Japanese.

"Among other things," Jason said. "He has his hands in quite a few pies. His loan business is mostly just a front, though. What he does is give people who are struggling financially a loan with enough money to pay off their debts, but they never realize that his loans have a high interest rate and hidden fees. Once their debt is paid off, they find themselves in debt to him. He gives them a deadline of when they need to begin paying off the loan, and when they can't, he seizes their property, then sells it to companies who are looking to expand their business." Jason paused, sighed, then leaned forward. "I hear he's already got a buyer for this place... some bigwig corporation who wants to turn this property into a catgirl bar."

Chris withheld his grimace, but the words were enough to make his stomach churn.

There were establishments like catgirl bars and strip clubs that thrived in certain areas of Los Angeles. They were considered legitimate business. While the government had tried shutting them down on occasion, it never really worked out because places like that made so much money. Money talked. In the end, all the government could do was set down stringent standards and policies regarding establishments like that. Chris remembered seeing a report on the news several years ago when this was a hot topic.

As he glanced at the doorway again, a fierce struggle waged within Chris's mind before he ultimately sighed. He really felt for this place, but he couldn't get involved with something like this. He had his own life to live, his own struggles to overcome, and really, he didn't even know if there was something he could do to help.

At the end of the day, Chris was just a college student attending a university to become a catgirl doctor. What could someone like him do against a person like this Calvin Lafaard? Not a damn thing. At least, that was what he told himself.

chapter 3

The day after he and Silva visited Kuro and the other catgirls at the orphanage, Chris woke up early in the morning and traveled to school after eating a… not-so-hearty breakfast of burnt eggs and salmon roe.

Silva had tried cooking breakfast. Chris had tried teaching her. Unfortunately, he'd let his attention slip during the lesson. He had come up behind her to give instructions, but she had pressed her deliciously small rump into his crotch and… well, one thing led to another and it ultimately ended with them burning the food. Silva had apologized several times, but it wasn't really her fault. He shouldn't have gotten so close to her while she was trying to cook.

As he sat in the lecture hall, his thoughts turned to Sister Ann and her situation.

Chris was completely positive there was nothing he could do to help her. He had no authority, no money, and no real knowledge of how loans worked, never mind how the mind of a loan shark operated. There were a lot of reasons why he couldn't help her. Honestly, it would probably make things worse.

But that didn't mean he didn't want to.

A big reason of why he wished he could help was because Kuro and the other catgirls who'd been with Silva were there. In fact, he would admit they were the biggest reason he wanted to help. If the orphanage went under and they were forced to move... well, he was sure they'd be placed in a government sanctioned orphanage or a community home for catgirls, but that would mean moving further away. The nearest community for catgirls was located in Los Angeles. It would take a long time to get there if Silva wanted to visit, which meant she wouldn't be able to see them as much.

"You look like you're deep in thought," a voice said in his ear.

Chris blinked several times as a blonde beauty entered his vision. She was wearing her usual fashionable clothes. Her yellow dress swished around her thighs as she walked, revealing beautifully long legs. A blue jacket went over the dress. Her hair had been styled in a ponytail near the back, but several bangs framed her face, highlighting her gorgeous blue eyes. He noticed she was wearing boots. It was an odd choice, but he felt it suited her ensemble.

The sweet scent of perfume drifted into his nose, causing him to shudder slightly. It was a new perfume that exuded a spicy and daring fragrance. He thought there was a hint of ginger, tuberose, and sandalwood. The combination was a little intoxicating.

"Anastasia?" he said in a questioning tone before shaking his head. He plastered on a smile and greeted the woman. "How was your weekend?"

"Busy." Anastasia huffed as she set her laptop bag on the table, plopped herself into the seat beside him, and removed her laptop from the case. "My mother is hosting a convention in downtown Los Angeles soon, and she's got me working day and night with the prep work."

"A convention, huh?" Chris paused as he realized something. "Speaking of parents, I really don't know what yours do?"

"What a coincidence. I don't know what yours do either." Anastasia beamed.

Chris laughed. "Fair enough. Honestly, my parents don't do much." He shrugged. "My dad works as a firefighter for the San Jose Fire Department, and my mom is a business analyst." He beamed back at the woman. "Your turn."

"My mother is a catgirl rights activist and actress, though I'd say she's more activist these days," Anastasia said. "She's been working heavily with various government groups and political affiliations to further the develop the rights and independence of catgirls. She's actually the reason why catgirls can now attend college. My parents are divorced, so I don't see my father anymore, but he's an independent movie director."

Immediately after hearing Anastasia talk about what her mother did, Chris finally figured out why she'd seemed so familiar upon hearing her name.

"Your mom is Monica Pierce!" he said, shocked. "The Monica Pierce who literally helped create the Catgirl Protection Bureau fifteen years ago?!"

"That is the one," Anastasia said with a nod. Something about the expression in her eyes told Chris he was treading murky waters. "At present, she is planning a four day convention with various political factions and support groups in an attempt to further her ambitions."

"Her... ambitions?" Chris asked, not quite sure what that meant.

"To further protect and nurture catgirls suffering from abuse is her current ambition," Anastasia said. "Though she is also working on stemming the growing slave market. I'm not sure if you know this, but catgirls sell at a very high price on the slave markets. Catgirl trafficking has currently reached an all-time high in the past two years."

Chris had not been aware of the numbers, but he did know about catgirl trafficking. There were a lot of people who wanted to own a catgirl slave. In fact, human trafficking had gone down simply because so many people wanted a catgirl. It was a disgusting practice that made Chris's entire body shimmer with barely contained rage when he thought about it, which was why he often tried not to think about it. He couldn't do anything to stop what was happening no matter how angry he got. Getting angry was an endeavor in futility.

"Your mom does some awfully important work," Chris said with admiration.

However, Anastasia scoffed. "She does indeed do a lot of important work. Her work is so important that she doesn't even have time to pay attention to her kids."

After she finished speaking, Chris knew he'd stumbled into a landmine, but Professor Shinomiya arrived before he could try to patch up the woman's delicate state of mind. He was left with no other choice but to turn away and begin writing notes as Professor Shinomiya began her lecture on how a cat's sense of taste and smell differed from a human's.

As the lecture continued, Chris found himself glancing at Anastasia out of the corner of his eye. She looked like she was diligently typing away on her computer. While studying her in profile, he wondered if he should talk to her after class. He'd been meaning to do so ever since he had lunch with her and her friends, but with everything that happened, he hadn't had the time.

However, he really should.

That was why, as class ended, he slung his backpack over his shoulder and turned to Anastasia as she was putting her laptop away.

"Do you have a moment? I'd like to talk to you about something."

Anastasia paused, laptop halfway into her case. Then she pushed the laptop in the case, zipped it up, and stood. She studied him with a passive gaze that felt like she was looking through him.

"Yeah. We can talk," she said at last. "I still have some time before my next class."

"Good. In that case, please follow me. We can talk over coffee."

There was a Starbucks located in the next building over. They ordered some drinks, a tall coffee with room for cream for Chris and a white mocha latté for Anastasia.

Chris never could drink his coffee black and always needed to add a lot of cream to overpower the bitterness of the coffee. His dad often made fun of him, calling him a ninny, but he simply wasn't a fan of bitter flavors. About the only thing he could eat that had a slight bitterness to it was dark chocolate.

"So, what did you want to talk about?" asked Anastasia as they sat down, drinks in hand.

"I'm not very good at this sort of thing, so I'm just going to come right out and ask." He stared at Anastasia, who seemed to sense something in his gaze and suddenly sat straighter. "Your friends said some interesting things when we all ate lunch together. Now, I could be reading too much into their words, but, well... do you like me? I mean, as more than just that random nice guy you sit next to in class?"

Chris didn't think Anastasia had been prepared for this question. It was a good thing she hadn't taken a drink of her latté yet, because he was sure she'd have choked or maybe even done a classic spit take.

"Well... well!" Anastasia began in a stuttering voice as though she wasn't sure how to begin. However, she eventually sighed, reached out to grab one of her bangs, and tugged on it. "I guess you *would* be curious about something like that after those idiots refused to shut their mouths." She paused, then sighed again. "Yes, I do like you. I wouldn't have asked you to take me out or been so forward if I didn't. Now that you know this, I'm wondering what you plan to do about it?"

She gave him a look that all but demanded an answer, and Chris knew better than to just leave the woman hanging. The entire reason he'd gone out of his way to speak with her was for this.

"I plan to politely turn you down," Chris said at last.

"I see." Anastasia narrowed her eyes. "It's that catgirl you are living with, isn't it?"

Chris tried not to shift uncomfortably, but it was hard to do under her gaze. "It is. Silva became my catpanion just a little while ago. We even went to the Catgirl Protection Bureau's Office of Catpanion and Child Registration to have official records on file."

While Chris wouldn't say he felt guilty about what he was telling Anastasia, as he didn't think he had anything to feel guilty for, he wouldn't lie and say he didn't feel bad. Anastasia had been nice to him since they started speaking. He appreciated her honest and forthright nature, and she'd helped him out a number of times now. It was hard not to feel bad after something like this.

"Honestly, I feel like I should have seen this coming when you came to me for advice." Anatasia sighed as her shoulders slumped. There was a self-deprecating smile on her face that looked out of place on such a beautiful woman. "It was pretty obvious to me that you care for this girl deeply. That should have been a sign right there. I guess it's true what they say: 'The apple doesn't fall far from the tree.'"

Her last statement confused Chris at first, but he was able to work out what she meant after a little while. It all made sense once he recalled that her parents were divorced.

"Your father cheated on your mother with a catgirl, didn't he?"

"You got it right on the first try. That's pretty impressive." Chris took a sip of his now lukewarm coffee as Anastasia furrowed her brow in thought. "It happened four years ago. I was sixteen at the time, and my mother's popularity in Hollywood had reached a peak. She'd starred in several blockbusters and was already well-known for her passionate support of catgirl rights. There wasn't a single person who didn't know about her. On the other hand, my father wasn't doing so well."

She paused, and her eyes became glazed over, as though she was remembering those times back then.

"I think my father felt inadequate next to my mother. She always did feel larger than life. While she was experiencing success in everything she did, my father was struggling to get his movies out there. He only managed to have one movie aired in theaters. It was for a single day and it didn't do well. It got terrible reviews and my father sunk into a great depression. Sadly, mother dearest was too busy with her own activities to notice."

The sights and sounds of people walking past their table as they spoke echoed back to him. He didn't know what anyone was saying, but most of his attention was on the woman before him. The scent of coffee beans permeated the air. It mixed in with Anastasia's perfume, which drifted to him as she crossed one leg over the other.

"I don't think I can really blame my father for what happened," Anastasia continued talking. "He was struggling, lonely, and met a catgirl who was more than willing to support him through his time of need. My mother is not a very supportive woman. She barely even noticed her husband's plight. Even now, she is more focused on her ambitions and goals than she is her own children, and this is after she and father got divorced. Even during the divorce process, my mother didn't seem to care that he cheated on her with a catgirl."

As he listened to her words, Chris found himself thankful that his family was so normal. His parents never had the kinds of problems Anastasia was talking about. They were supportive, loved each other, and helped each other. Cliché as it sounded, they were a unit. Back when he was younger, Chris found that annoying, but now he could appreciate how much their presence had helped steady the other.

"Do you hate catgirls?" he asked suddenly.

"No, of course not." Anastasia shook her head. "I wouldn't be going to college to get a doctorate in Catgirl Psychology if I hated them."

"Sorry," he said. "You make a good point. I just figured…"

"You figured that since my father was stolen away by a catgirl and my mother loves catgirls so much she'd neglect her children that I must hate them, right?" When Chris fell silent, unable to say anything in his defense, she gave him a bitter smile. "It is true that I don't really like catgirls, but I'm not so cruel that I'd blame them for what happened to my parents. Even if catgirls didn't exist, I'm sure my parents would have ended up the same way. Blaming catgirls for their issues would be irresponsible."

"I suppose you have a point," Chris said slowly. "Still, given everything that happened, I'm a little surprised you're studying to become a catgirl doctor."

"I'm mostly doing this because I have to do something." Anastasia shrugged. "I don't particularly care about becoming a catgirl doctor or not, but I thought if I studied catgirls more in depth, it would help me understand them better. I thought if I could understand them, maybe I'd be able to learn why my mom is so intent on helping them."

"Do you think you understand them better now?" asked Chris.

"Not in the least," Anastasia admitted with a bitter smile.

***

Chris arrived at his apartment after pounding several punching bags and working up a good burn as he thought about everything he'd learned from Anastasia.

He wasn't sure where he stood with that girl anymore. Until now, Anastasia had been talking to him because she was interested in him as a potential boyfriend, but he had pumped that ship so full of holes he was certain it had already sunk to the Mariana Trench. Now that he'd done this, he didn't know if they could go back to being friends.

As he entered through the front door, Chris slipped off his shoes as Silva greeted him.

"Chris! Welcome home!"

"I'm home."

With a smile on his face, Chris looked up at Silva as she walked over to him with delicate footsteps and a gentle smile, but he paused when he noticed Kuro sitting on the couch and eyeing him like he was a criminal suspect. Her arm was still in a sling.

Silva didn't even seem to notice Kuro's glare as she leaned on her tiptoes, placed her hands on his chest, and kissed Chris on the lips. The floral scent of her shampoo and soap mixed with her delicate natural scent and intoxicated him even more than Anastasia's perfume. Her lips were impeccably soft. Honestly, if it wasn't because he could feel Kuro's glare on him, he would have taken this several steps further.

Just because the dark-skinned woman made him wary didn't mean Chris would not kiss back. He leaned into Silva's mouth and enjoyed the taste of her sweet lips. When he pulled back, however, he went back to eyeing Kuro.

"I didn't realize you knew where we lived," he said.

"Silva gave me your address, so I decided to stop by." Kuro shrugged, then gave him a look that clearly said she didn't trust him. "I hope that's not a problem."

"It's not." Chris assured her even though he was pretty wary of that glare. To get his mind off the look she was giving him, he glanced at Silva. "Should I get started on dinner?"

"Um, could I help?" asked Silva, twiddling her fingers as she looked at him. Her pleading expression, complete with jutting out lower lip, was absolutely adorable. Even though he remembered what happened this morning, Chris found it impossible to tell her no.

"Yeah, you can help me. We're making basic chicken and rice. How does that sound?"

Silva's bright eyes were practically glowing as she nodded several times. "Just tell me what to do!"

There were a number of chicken and rice recipes. All of them were also fairly easy to make. The one Chris had Silva help him make was a chicken and rice bake with cream of mushroom soup.

He had Silva preheat the oven to 375 degrees while he stirred the soup, water, rice, paprika, and black pepper in a baking dish. While he did this, Silva watched him with tentative eyes. He even caught her mimicking his hand movements as if she was shadow cooking.

While they cooked dinner, Kuro sat by the couch and watched TV. That was what it seemed like at first anyway. Chris caught her staring at him and Silva any number of times when he looked in her direction, but she would look away every time she realized she'd been found out.

It took 45 minutes to prepare the dinner and another 10 before it could be served. Silva set the dinner table and had Kuro come over as he placed the baking pan on top of the table and served them each a healthy portion.

Despite looking like she wanted to continue glaring at him, Kuro could not help but eye the food he'd prepared with glazed over eyes. She looked hungry as she licked her lips, perhaps unconsciously, and Chris tried his hardest not to smile.

"You don't need to stand on ceremony," he said. "Feel free to dig in."

Silva was the first to begin eating. She scooped a spoonful of rice and placed it in her mouth, purring in delight as the creamy rice hit her tongue. Chris also enjoyed the simple flavor. Kuro took a bit more time before trying her first bite, but once she tasted it, the woman ended up scarfing down his food as if it would disappear if she didn't eat fast enough.

As they ate, he and Silva talked.

"This food is a lot easier to make than the stuff Chef Gordon cooks."

"Chef Gordon is also a professional who creates dishes fit for wealthy elites who pay hundreds of dollars for a single meal."

"Do you think he ever makes anything like this?"

"I don't know, but I imagine he has a cooking channel where he makes stuff that even someone who doesn't have hundreds of dollars to spend on a single dish can cook."

"I should see if I can find it."

As he and Silva created a nice atmosphere with light conversation, Kuro took on a weird expression. Her frown seemed confused. She stared at Silva like she was seeing this girl for the first time.

After dinner, Silva had Chris and Kuro sit on the couch, then turned the television onto her favorite cooking show and promptly placed her hand on Chris's lap. When he felt her weight on his thighs, he couldn't help but chuckle as he reached out and began tenderly running his fingers through her hair and rubbing her ears. Silva purred as she closed her eyes and her breathing evened. She had fallen asleep.

Kuro had watched this whole process take place. Her face retained that odd expression, like she wasn't sure how she should take this. However, she eventually sighed.

"It seems Silva has really fallen head over heels for you," she said at last.

"I... guess so?" Chris wasn't sure what he should say to that.

"I told Silva I came over here to visit her, but the truth is that I wanted to check you out," Kuro continued. "There are a lot of people out there who abuse catgirls. I needed to make sure you weren't one of those people who pretends to be kind and compassionate but is secretly heartless and cruel."

"I understand," Chris said. "You didn't trust me."

"Don't misunderstand me," Kuro said. "It's not that I didn't trust you specifically. It's that I don't trust men in general. A lot of men act respectful and kind when they are in public and have completely different personalities in private. Some men don't even act nice in public. Markus was just one man in a long list of men who have abused catgirls for a long time. I had to be sure you weren't like them."

If she was that determined to check Chris out and make sure he was on the up and up, then Silva must have been very important to her, or maybe Kuro was just one of those protective types. He wasn't sure he could blame her for that.

"And what do you think now that you've seen me again?" asked Chris.

"I don't know." Kuro's frown deepened further. "You certainly seem like a good person, and you've obviously treated Silva well since she began living with you, but I feel like it's still too soon for me to trust you with her."

"Then what do you plan on doing?" asked Chris.

Kuro was silent for awhile. She looked down at Silva, whose head still rested in Chris's lap. The silver-haired catgirl's ears were twitching as she nuzzled her face against his thighs, forcing Chris to shift so she wouldn't accidentally give him an erection. He was sure Kuro would not appreciate seeing him grow aroused.

"I'll probably visit you more often and check in to see how Silva is doing until I'm satisfied you're not a threat."

Upon hearing her words, Chris could have done any number of things. He could have gotten angry at her lack of trust, could have thrown a fit or said something sarcastic, or given any other number of negative reactions. Having someone distrust him this much did rankle on his nerves. Yet he also understood where she was coming from.

Kuro and Silva had both been abused by their guardian, physically, mentally, emotionally, and sexually. They had undergone hardships he couldn't even imagine. With her past as the only guide she could use to move forward, it was only obvious that Kuro would distrust someone she didn't know. Chris couldn't blame her for that.

Even if it did annoy him.

"In that case, I can give you a spare key to the apartment," Chris said.

Kuro looked nonplussed. "You would do that?"

"If you're going to come over whenever you want anyways, I might as well." Shrugging, Chris considered her for a moment, then looked down at Silva and added. "Besides, it would be nice if Silva had someone she could talk to when I'm not around. I'm always gone for several hours each day, so she has to be bored remaining cooped up in here all day." He smiled when, upon rubbing the inside of her left ear, Silva released a delicate purr and curled her toes in pleasure. "Maybe you could even consider going outside with her. I don't think it's healthy to remain indoors constantly, but I'd be worried for her safety if she went out by herself."

Silva had been getting a lot better about not panicking when they went outside, so he was sure she'd be okay traveling around so long as there was someone who could look after her. He didn't know Kuro very well. However, merely from her physically imposing stature, Chris knew she would be able to keep any people from giving Silva unwanted advances. He was certain she'd be able to protect Silva from potential danger.

"I really don't understand you," Kuro admitted after staring at him for a number of minutes.

"What don't you understand?" asked Chris.

"I've treated you with suspicion this entire time, and yet despite this, you're not only okay with me coming over, but you're going to give me a spare key to your house? That doesn't make sense."

"Try to look at this from my perspective," Chris said. "I've got a catgirl who doesn't trust me, but she clearly loves my catpanion a lot and is very protective over her. Silva trusts you, and I am fairly certain you wouldn't do anything to harm her. That's why I'm willing to extend my trust to you, even if you don't trust me back."

"Hmph. You're pretty good at using logic and words to win arguments, aren't you?" asked Kuro. She looked like she wanted to cross her arms, but one of them was in a sling.

When she remembered this, she scowled and set her other arm on her lap.

"Isn't that how someone always wings an argument? With logic and words?" When Kuro's scowl deepened, he chuckled just a little before gesturing to her arm. "By the way, what happened?"

"This?" Kuro glanced at her arm before a fierce grin split her face. "It's a memento from when I attacked Markus. He ended up getting a good shot off and got me in the shoulder." She paused. "You wanna see the wound?"

As the woman grinned at him, Chris could admit, if only to himself, that there was something innately sexy about a strong woman with muscles. It was a different sort of attractiveness from Silva. His catpanion was cute and innocent, but those traits gave her a quality that he could only call adorably seductive. Her innocent expressions when she was sucking him off or when he went down on her, lapping at her pussy as she released her juices into his mouth, turned him on so much. However, seeing a strong and muscular woman like Kuro grinning at him with that fiercely joyful and triumphant expression was a different kind of turn on.

He honestly couldn't say which he liked more.

"Can I?" he asked.

"I don't mind." Kuro shrugged, and then proceeded to remove a part of her shirt so he could see the ugly bullet wound underneath. It was a lighter area than the rest of her skin.

"That's quite the battle scar," he said.

"Hmph. It's just one of many," Kuro retorted as she pulled her muscles shirt back up, concealing the wound.

The rest of Kuro's time was spent telling Chris about how she'd beaten Markus into submission despite nearly passing out from bloodloss.

It was… quite enlightening.

chapter 4

Ever since Chris gave Kuro a spare key to his apartment, the woman had begun spending more and more time at his place. While he did think this was a good thing because it made Silva happy, he also thought it was a problem because he and Silva had not been able to have sex for several days. He'd given her that key as a gesture of good faith. However, while Chris wasn't sure about this, it seemed like Kuro was using her privilege to cockblock him.

Several days without being able to have sex was maddening.

Chris had considered revoking her privileges and taking the keys back, but she technically hadn't done anything wrong. She just showed up at the exact moment he and Silva were about to get it on.

Like this one time when he and Silva were making out on the couch, his hands in her pants and he was massaging her ass. Kuro had shown up just as Silva had pulled down their pants and got ready to insert his dick in her pussy. She'd apologized and said to continue before leaving, but the mood had been thoroughly ruined.

And that wasn't the only time she had interrupted them. Just the other day, he and Silva had decided to try doing it 69. It had been a lot of fun. Chris still remembered the feeling of Silva's rough tongue as she licked his dick like it was a lollipop. She'd even gone a step further and began suckling on his balls as she stroked his saliva covered shaft. Chris had not only immensely enjoyed the sensations, but he had loved the way her pussy trembled when he snuck his tongue into her folds and played with her clit.

It had been an amazing experience, and he and Silva had come so close to getting that sweet, sweet release... and then Kuro had barged into their bedroom with the subtlety of a jackhammer pounding pavement. Her entrance had basically been like dropping a bucket of water from the arctic onto their heads. Even now he could remember the embarrassing way his dick had shriveled in Silva's mouth.

That was one of the more humiliating moments he had experienced.

He really wanted to get back at Kuro for that.

Humiliating experiences aside, Silva did appreciate the extra company, so Chris was putting up with the women for now, though he might not depending on how long this situation lasted.

Of course, at present, he was venting all those emotions into his exercise.

Chris took a quick step forward, unleashed a quick jab with his right hand, then pulled back and released a left hook. His opponent and sparring partner blocked the jab with his left hand and avoided the hook by leaning back. He growled as he watched Tanner shuffle away from him with ease. The man was quite fleet-footed despite being so large.

While Tanner was quick on his feet, Chris was no slouch either. He followed the man step for step, launching several jabs before throwing a kick to his opponent's thigh. A loud thud rang out as Tanner lifted his leg and blocked the kick with his shin. Chris clicked his tongue and moved back to put some distance between them.

Their sparring had been going on for quite a while now. Chris wasn't sure how long, but his breathing had become quite heavy and a sharp ache filled his chest when he breathed in. Then again, that might have just been from when Tanner struck his side with a sharp hit. That punch had rattled his ribcage a bit.

Some sweat got into Chris's eyes, forcing him to blink, and in that time Tanner rushed forward and appeared in front of him. The man was already throwing a powerful straight punch. He was rotating his entire body to put more force into this attack. Chris felt a jolt run through him as he twisted his body to avoid the punch and launched a counter punch, though it was blocked with a forearm. A loud thudding noise echoed from the point of impact and spread across the kickboxing center.

"Let's stop here for today," Tanner said as he stepped back. Like Chris, the man was drenched in sweat, shirting sticking to his dark skin as the veins on his arms and chest stood out.

"Sounds good... to me..." Chris said, far more out of breath than Tanner. He glared resentfully at the man. Damn ex-Marine and his insane freaking stamina.

They sat together on a bench as Chris uncapped his water bottle and took a large swig of Gatorade. He guzzled the liquid down like drinking was going out of style. Sighing in relief after he'd had his fill, he screwed the cap back on and watched as two people entered the ring he and Tanner had just left.

"So how's mated life?" Tanner asked, his manner joking.

"Mated life" was a joking term among men who were romantically involved with catgirls. It referred to men who had catpanions. Having a catpanion was not the same as marriage, but it came with similar benefits. Because it wasn't legally recognized as marriage—due to the influence of several political factions that were against giving catgirls the right to marry—it was often referred to as being mated, since the humans involved with them were essentially a catgirl's mate.

"It's fine… though I could do without her friend barging in on us," Chris said.

"You should consider taking a firmer stand," Tanner said. "This woman sounds like a real piece of work."

"She is, but she's also Silva's best friend." Chris ran a hand through his sweaty hair. He ignored the slick feeling on his palm and fingers as he placed his hands on the bench. "I can't exactly kick her out, nor do I want to. I just want her to not abuse the key I gave her. It was something I gave her out of trust, and I feel like that trust is being abused."

"Well, knowing you, I'm sure you'll think of something," Tanner said.

After their conversation, Chris took a quick shower and walked home. When he arrived at his apartment, it was to find Kuro thankfully not present, and Silva standing in the kitchen and wearing an apron. An appetizing scent drifted through the air. As he took several whiffs, Chris smelled something baking. There was a hint of citrus to the scent, which caused his stomach to rumble.

"Chris, welcome home!" Silva said with a bright smile. She looked his way, but quickly turned her attention back to the food.

"I'm home," Chris said in response.

After slipping off his shoes, he walked into the kitchen and began getting out the plates and utensils. He'd noticed that Silva hadn't set the table yet. He also grabbed the place mats and some napkins.

"Is that breaded tilapia?" he asked as he went about setting the table.

"It is!" Silva nodded, an enthusiastic smile on her face. "I noticed that we had some in the fridge, so I grabbed the bread crumbs, Parmesan cheese, garlic salt, and lemon peel to make it. I did have to use the last of the butter, though."

"We'll have to go shopping soon anyway," Chris said. "We can do that this weekend."

"Okay!"

A few minutes after Chris finished setting the table, Silva removed the baking tray from the oven. Chris arrived with the plates and had her scoop the tilapia onto each one. The breaded fish were a light brown color, and when he took a fork to them, they flaked apart easily, showing they had been thoroughly cooked through.

Chris took his first bite after they sat down to eat and nearly gasped. The breading was nice and crunchy. Meanwhile, the fish was juicy and moist but had been thoroughly cooked. The Parmesan cheese mixed with the lemon peel added a nice flavor that complimented each other well.

"This is delicious," he mumbled.

"Thank you!" Silva beamed.

"You've become quite the chef."

"Meow... I just follow the directions."

"That's half the battle right there. Too many people don't follow the directions. I knew this one person who liked getting 'creative' with their dishes and always ended up making something that could be classified as a Weapon of Mass Destruction."

"This person sounds dangerous."

"Very dangerous."

They continued to converse until the food was finished. Since Silva had done the cooking, Chris took care of the dishes. His homework was already finished. That meant he could relax. When the dishes were all clean, he joined Silva on the couch and snuggled with her until late at night.

After brushing their teeth, Chris and Silva lay in bed. The warmth from Silva's skin and the softness of her chest on his made him remember how he'd been complaining about his lack of sex. As if these thoughts were spurning him on, Chris slid his hand down Silva's back, until he was cupping her rear end.

"I don't want to go to sleep," Chris said finally.

"T-that's good. I don't really want to sleep right now either," Silva stuttered as a soft purring emitted from her throat. Her butt cheeks were softer than anything he'd ever felt. He loved how his hands sank into the soft skin of her pert ass.

Silva climbed up Chris until she was straddling his leg. He felt her pussy press down on his leg, leaving a wet trail as she ground her aroused nether lips against him. The way her stomach moved with the actions was like an erotic dance. Her small breasts jiggled as well, resulting in his cock becoming increasing stiff.

She leaned forward and kissed him, her hands making a mess of his hair as her small tongue probed his mouth. She was being much more aggressive than normal. As the sensations of her tongue entwining with his ran through him, Chris wondered if maybe she was feeling as frustrated by their lack of sex as he was.

As they kissed, Chris reached for her breasts with one hand and cupped her sex with the other. Silva mewled as he rubbed his index finger along her outer labia. His index finger came away covered in juices. He pushed his hand against her again, inserting a single finger, which caused Silva to buck as she slid her hands down his stomach, trailing over his abs before wrapping her delicate hands around his throbbing dick.

"It's so hot," she murmured between kisses. "Your dick is like a furnace."

"If it's hot, then it's because you made it that way," Chris said in reply, even though it made no sense.

"I want it in me. I want it in me so bad," Silva moaned as Chris used his thumb to rub her clit. The bundle of nerves twitched underneath his ministrations. Her thighs were quivering by this point.

"In that case, you should put it in."

"B-behind. Do me from behind," Silva moaned as she removed herself from him. She turned around and leaned on her chest and stomach, waving her butt in the air. Her tail was raised high, allowing him to easily see her dripping wet pussy. Juices were mixing with sweat along her thighs, creating glistening trails on her skin.

Chris stood on his knees and walked over, placing a hand on either side of her hips as he lined up his dick with her entrance. He didn't push it in at first. Instead, he rubbed his cock against her pussy, coating it in a nice layer of her juices. Silva's ass trembled and shook as though she was being rocked by miner spasms.

"Mreow... d-don't tease me please," she gasped, back arching.

"Sorry. That wasn't my intention," Chris said.

"Please... just put it in. Put it in now."

Despite her words, Chris still didn't insert his dick right away. He studied Silva from behind. Her small round ass was incredibly cute, but when combined with her dripping snatch and puffy pussy lips, it created an image that would have made any man harder than a rock. He followed her thighs down to her cute little feet. Her toes were clenching as if waiting for him to screw her from behind. Then he followed his gaze along the curvature of her spine, all the way to her slender shoulders and neck. Long silver hair spread out like a curtain around her. It shimmered in the moonlight and created an enchanting image of sensuality that made his dick twitch as blood surged through it.

Finally, after catching this amazing glimpse of perfection, Chris lined himself up and pushed his dick into her pussy. The ridges of her walls tightly embraced him. He groaned as the feeling of being squeezed through a tube came over him, but it wasn't unpleasant. Silva was just tight. Her pussy was like a vice, but it was one he was more than happy to be trapped in.

He retracted his hips and thrust them forward. The sound of his hips and balls slapping against her echoed all around them, but it was overpowered by Silva's loud "Mreow!" as she arched her spine and stretched her hands out in front of her. Chris worked in a steady pace, doing his best to alternative how he moved based on the noises she made. Silva was a very vocal lover, so he knew when he was doing something right.

"Mreow! Meow! Mew! Mreoooowww!"

Chris bit his lips as he felt his balls contracting, struggling to keep himself from cumming. He wanted to cum so bad. How long had it been? Honestly, he didn't think it had been that long since Kuro had only began showing up, but even so, it felt like it had been way too long since he'd been able to fuck this pussy.

And yet, as if God himself was against Chris finishing, the sound of a door opening echoed to him in the room. Mere moments later, Kuro burst in.

"Hey, you two! What are you—"

She paused. Her eyes grew cold when she saw what they were doing. However, she also looked conflicted.

"Why are you stopping?" Silva complained.

"Uh… well, Kuro is…"

"I don't care what Kuro is doing," Silva said, her voice unusually passionate. "I want this! Chris! Don't stop! Please don't stop!"

Chris was conflicted. He was still harder than a rock, but Kuro was right there, staring at him as he was buried to the hilt inside of Silva's tight little pussy. He was fucking Kuro's friend right in front of her.

Actually, now that he was thinking about it, the idea of someone else watching him have sex was kind of turning him on. The last time this happened, his dick had shriveled up from embarrassment. Now, however... well, he kind of wanted to get back at this woman for her cockblocking and felt like this was the perfect revenge.

"Mreow! Y-you're getting bigger!" Silva ground her backside against him, which caused Chris to groan as lightning traveled from his cock straight to his brain. "Oh, God! You're getting bigger! Please! Do me! Meow! I need it right meow!"

Hearing Silva so passionately declare that she needed him to fuck her was his breaking point. Chris didn't hesitate any longer. He leaned down, wrapped his arms around Silva's waist, and pulled her backwards. Chris fell onto his back, hitting the pillows as he began thrusting his dick inside of her from this new angle. Silva screamed.

"Oh! So good! So! Yes! This is it! Chris! I love you! I love you!"

"I… love you… too!"

Chris couldn't fully form words as he was busy pounding into Silva from behind. Instead of just saying it, Chris tried to show Silva how much he loved her by leaning down to press his lips against the sweat spot on her neck. Silva released several louder moans that mixed in with the lewd noises as his cock churned her insides. Not only did Chris begin sucking and kissing her neck, but he removed his hands from her waist and began massaging her tits. He pinched her nipples between his fingers, tugging on them. It wasn't a hard tug, but it was enough that Silva arched her spine and released a loud mewl that he was sure the neighbors could hear.

And then it was over. Chris felt an indescribable moment where the entire world seemed to be overloaded with white. Pleasure like never before raced through his cock as his balls and abdomen swelled with pressure, and then he was releasing his seed inside of Silva's pussy. There was so much he could actually feel the mixture of their cum spilling out of her and drenching their thighs.

As he came inside of her, Silva released a loud "MREOW!!" as her walls tightened around him. Her body shook and shuddered. Her thighs clenched and trembled. Chris reached over as Silva orgasmed and placed his fingers on her clit, which he rubbed furiously, causing Silva to have a second orgasm immediately after the first.

Then they were both done. He pulled out his cock with a wet plop that sounded abnormally loud in the now still room. As he did, he glanced at Silva, who lay with her back pressed against his chest. She had become boneless. Her body was looked like a soggy noodle covered in a layer of water. Her skin glistened with sweat. She had shut her eyes already, and he could see from the rise and fall of her chest that she'd gone completely to sleep.

Chris was barely able to remain awake as well, eyes closing against his will. With the last of his strength, he cast a glance toward where he had seen Kuro, but the woman was no longer there.

***

Kuro did not show up for several days after she watched Chris and Silva having sex. If Chris was being honest with himself, he was a little embarrassed when he finally realized what he'd done. Kuro had caught him and Silva on the verge of having sex several times, true, but they had never gone all the way, and they certainly hadn't kept going after she interrupted them.

The other night must have just been their final straw. There was only so much cockblocking they could take before issues like being caught in the throes of passion no longer mattered.

At least, that was what he told himself.

Life continued on as usual before Kuro had entered it. While he didn't mind this completely, as it meant he and Silva could have all the sex they wanted, he was disheartened because Silva expressed sorrow at the other catgirl disappearing again. The look on her face had been enough to make Chris consider traveling to the orphanage just to bring Kuro back. Unfortunately, he still had classes and couldn't do that until this weekend.

Of course, all that changed a few days later.

***

Chris was relaxing as he sat on a bench and rested his sore muscles. He'd pushed himself a fair bit harder that day than normal. It felt like he had not only pushed his body but also his mind. An Internal conflict had taken place inside of him, between going after Kuro and bringing her back over to letting her stay away, and he had finally settled on what he was going to do.

He was going to visit the orphanage again.

Regardless of anything else, Kuro was important to Silva, and she was therefore important to him. He would talk to her and convince the catgirl to start visiting once more.

Those were Chris's thoughts until the door to the kickboxing center opened and a woman walked in. Tall and muscular, with gorgeous dark skin, a lean waist, and a massive rack, the woman looked like a predator as she walked forward. She was wearing military fatigues that day. A small hole in the back allowed her black tail to spring free, while the ears on her head twitched several times.

While the other people inside of the training center gawked in surprise at this gorgeous catgirl who looked like an Amazonian queen, Chris gawked for a different reason.

"Kuro?" He rubbed his eyes to see if he was hallucinating. Nope. She was still there. "What are you doing here?"

Kuro stopped in front of him, her figure so much taller that she could tower over him with ease. Her glare was not hard or filled with anger. However, there was a fire in her eyes that he hadn't seen before. He didn't know what it was, but he recognized the determination blazing inside of those enthralling green irises.

"You. Me. In the ring. Now."

"Huh?" Chris gave the woman his most eloquent response. It took him several seconds to figure out what she was saying. "You... want to spar with me?"

"That's what I just said," she replied, rolling her eyes.

"Why?" Chris couldn't help but ask.

"I'm not good with words," Kuro said. "I can't understand people or trust the words they speak, and I can't speak in a way that people can easily understand. Since I'm no good with talking, I'm going to let my fists do the talking."

"Let your fists... you want us to communicate through our fists?" asked Chris.

Kuro shrugged. "It worked for Kevin and Justin."

"Huh." Chris scratched his head. "Didn't know you were a reader."

"I've only read a few books." Kuro crossed her arms. "Are we going to do this or not?"

"Yeah. Sure. Why not?"

Chris couldn't think of any reason not to do this... other than he was sore, tired, and just wanted to go home and bury his face between Silva's legs. However, aside from those reasons, he didn't have any to refuse her.

They stepped onto the ring. Chris put his kickboxing gloves back on. Meanwhile, Kuro wrapped her hands in bandages before sliding on a pair of boxing gloves that Tanner gave her. After he did this, the big black man meandered over to Chris and leaned down.

"This the woman who kept cock blocking you?" he asked.

"Yeup," Chris muttered.

"Damn, son. You are shit out of luck."

"Gee." Chris scowled at the man. "Thanks."

He pounded his gloves together as Kuro got into position, sliding her feet apart as she adopted a stance he didn't recognized. Her hands were out in front of her, just below her chin, but they were... curved? It looked like her hands were bent to form a paw instead of a fist, which looked awkward with the gloves on. Despite how silly the position seemed, Chris was certain he couldn't underestimate this woman. Those muscles didn't look like they were just for show.

Tanner was the one who signaled the start to this impromptu match. The moment he shouted "start!", Kuro shoved off with her right foot and blitzed toward Chris. She was so fast Chris barely had time to move out of the way before she was on him. Her fist—paw?—swiped through the air, cutting through where he'd been just moments before.

Despite missing, Kuro didn't let up. She snapped her left foot forward in a sharp kick that would have caught him in the shin if he hadn't raised his leg to avoid it. Stepping on the ground after her kick failed, Kuro surged forward like a jaguar, throwing a series of straight jabs with both hands. Left. Right. One. Two. Each punch felt like it was slicing through the atmosphere, producing a loud whistling noise that alarmed Chris and made him stumble.

While Chris was surprised, he had no intention of letting her get the better of him forever. Chris watched her every move, cataloging which foot she preferred to lead with, which hand she threw her first combo with, and what sort of attacks she used. She led with her left foot, attacked with her right fist, and favored moving left when she was circling him.

Once he felt like he had her rhythm down, Chris stepped forward and threw two punches. Both were blocked. The dull thud of his boxing gloves echoing off her forearms resounded around them. Kuro narrowed her eyes and countered with a series of lightning fast punches, but she had a slight disadvantage when it came to close-range attacks. Chris was smaller and more nimble than her. While her attacks were fast and powerful, they were easier to dodge from up close.

Thud! Thud!

Finally, Chris got two good hits in. However, those hits felt a lot like striking steel with his bare hand. He gawked as he moved back, dodged left to avoid her next attack, and put some distance between them.

"Woman! What the hell are you made of?!" he squawked.

"Just flesh and blood," said Kuro.

"I'm not buying that! Your stomach is like steel!"

Kuro gave him an alluring yet predatory smile, as if he had just paid her the greatest compliment imaginable. She licked her lips. Those lush lips. For a moment, Chris actually found himself jealous, though whether he was jealous of her tongue or her lips was an entirely different matter. That said, part of him wondered what it would feel like to lick those lips.

Why was he thinking about this again?

Just as Chris was dispelling those odd but arousing thoughts, Kuro came in again. She lunged forward faster than he anticipated and threw a punch. He dodged, but then Kuro did something he didn't expect, dropping to the ground and throwing out a low-kick that caught his legs. The strength of her kick was incredible. Chris was swept off his feet with ease. He struck the ring, coughing and gasping as the wind was knocked from his lungs.

Chris didn't even have time to recover before Kuro was straddling him. As he felt her hot body come into contact with his hips, a jolt raced through him.

"Ha... ha..."

Kuro placed her hands on either side of his head as she leaned over, her breathing deep, heavy, and her dark cheeks flushed. Her forehead had a light layer of sweat covering it. The glossy sheen it produced enhanced her already attractive but feral features. As he stared at her glowing viridian eyes, lush lips, and flushed cheeks, Chris felt an undeniable attraction that he nevertheless resisted.

After all, Silva was his catpanion. He wouldn't betray her.

"You..." Kuro finally spoke.

"Me?" Chris asked.

"You are a very good man. I can tell from our fight that you're very protective of others. Even though I was fighting seriously, you didn't attack to injure but to disable. I can see why Silva loves you so much." She smiled, then looked away as if suddenly feeling awkward. "In any case... I've actually... been trying to apologize. I know I was being rude when I kept barging into your love nest like that."

"I'm not sure I would call our apartment a love nest..." Chris muttered.

Kuro continued on as if she hadn't heard him. "Actually, I knew you were a good man a few days after we met. You didn't get upset at me, even though I prevented you and Silva from having sex, but I've... well..."

When Kuro trailed off, Chris realized that whatever she wanted from him, it wasn't what she'd originally said. Her bogus story about communicating through their fists had been complete bullcrap. However, now that he had realized this, he was wondering what, exactly, she wanted from him.

"It's hard for me to ask this of you." Kuro licked her lips again, but it was a nervous gesture this time. "I've run into a problem that I can't solve by myself. I was thinking of ways to ask for your help, but..."

"But?" Chris asked when Kuro trailed off.

"But I hate debasing myself in front of others to ask for help," Kuro admitted.

And just like that, like lightning flashing through his mind, Chris realized why Kuro had fought him.

"Kuro..." he began, a suspicious tone in his voice. "Is the reason you fought and pinned me to the ground like this because you want to ask me for something, but your pride won't allow you to ask for anything, so you've pinned me here to try and demand I help you?"

"No, no, no." Kuro waved her hands back and forth. He wondered if she knew she was still straddling him. "I wasn't going to demand your help. I just needed... to release stress before I could properly ask you for help. I promise. I'm not the kind of cat who would demand someone help them with her problem."

"I see." Chris considered what she said for a moment, then decided to just accept her words at face value. He was too tired to do anything otherwise. "Well, in that case, I guess we could go back to my place and talk."

"Yes, please," Kuro said immediately. She seemed a little too eager. "Silva should hear this as well."

"All right. Well, that's fine and all, but…"

Kuro tilted her head. "What is it?"

"Could you get off me?" asked Chris, his cheeks burning as he looked away.

Kuro didn't understand at first, but then she shifted and felt something hard poking at her through his pants. She looked down, saw the object straining against his shorts, and squawked as she leapt to her feet. For the first time ever, Chris finally got to see her blush. He probably would have found that amusing, but a lot of the people who went to this kickboxing center were now point and gawking at his erection. He did his best to hide it, but, well, there was no hiding that.

His cheeks burned. How shameful.

chapter 5

"Right. *The guide to cooking a perfect steak. Hot pan. The secret here is to make sure we literally sear the steak and not broil it. Season it first."*

Silva hummed to herself, tail lightly swishing as she listened to Chef Ramsay impart pearls of cooking wisdom. She couldn't see what he was doing because she was in the kitchen, but she listened to what he was telling her, heating up the pan on the electric stove, grabbing a bit of pink Himalayan salt and sprinkling it over the two steaks.

The cuts she was using were sirloin. She and Chris had bought them the other day when they went grocery shopping.

"Get some nice, large grains of pepper, so you've got a nice bit of heat."

Grabbing the pepper grinder, she twisted the bottom part —she didn't know what it was called—and let grains of pepper fall out and onto the steaks, which sat on a wooden cutting board. After which, just like Chef Ramsay said to do, she mopped up the seasoning, then added some oil onto the pan and moved it around. Finally, she put the steaks down, laying them away from her.

Almost immediately after placing the steaks in the pan, a loud sizzling sound emitted from them. She didn't let this startle her. According to Chef Ramsay, this was how it was supposed to sound. She used tongs to flip the steaks over. The bottom side, now the top side, had a nice golden brown color. After a moment, she placed them on their backs near the edge of the pan and tilted the pan to let the fats sear the steak even better. After searing the backs, she crushed some garlic and added it to the steak, then added some thyme followed by more olive oil, and finally butter.

Once she added the butter, Silva began basting the steaks, making sure the butter soaked into the steak. She rubbed the thyme and garlic over it to add more flavor. As she did, the mouth-watering scent of the seared steaks mixed with butter, garlic, and thyme and filled the air. Her mouth watered and her stomach rumbled. She shook her head and slapped her cheeks.

"Don't drool. You have to control yourself, Silva. W-wait until Chris comes home before eating... m-maybe I can have a bite—no, no. Wait until Chris comes home."

As Silva debated with herself, she took the steaks off the pan and placed them on the cutting board. The scent wafting from them really did make her mouth water. She wanted more than anything to take one of those steaks and sink her fangs into it, but that would have been bad manners.

To distract herself, Silva tossed together a quick salad in a bowl using the lettuce they had in the fridge and mixed it with some other vegetables like carrots. She also added some olive oil, vinegar, and some dijon mustard, which she mixed together, and then sprinkled a pinch of salt and pepper over the whole thing.

"Done!"

Silva clapped her hands together, feeling rather proud of herself. It had been a really long time since she watched her Grams cook. She remembered how much Grams had loved cooking, and she had even been allowed to help on occasion. Those had been some of her happiest moments, and they were now her fondest memories. This was actually why she wanted to learn how to cook, to recapture the times she spent with her Grams.

At that moment, the door finally opened and a voice sounded out.

"I'm home!"

"Ah!" Silva wiped her hands on her apron and went to the entrance. She hoped he would like her outfit. "Welcome home... Chris..." She paused when her eyes landed on the dark-skinned woman with him. "Kuro? What are you doing here?"

Kuro eyed Silva for a long moment, glancing down at her bare feet before trailing an incredulous gaze along the rest of her body. Silva felt an intense moment of discomfort. Her cheeks began burning as Kuro finally looked her in the eyes.

"Never mind what I'm doing here. What are you wearing?"

"A-an apron," Silva mumbled.

"Yes, I can see that. What I mean is: Why are you wearing nothing but an apron?"

Indeed, Silva had opted to wear an apron and nothing else. She was completely naked underneath it. If she were to turn around right now, Chris and Kuro would have gotten an eye full of her backside.

"N-no reason. I'm, um, I'm just... going to get dressed. Dinner is ready, but I haven't set the table yet."

"I'll set the table," Chris said as he looked at Silva with a gaze that made her heat up. That hungry look was what she had been hoping to see, but now she couldn't even enjoy it. She was happy Kuro had decided to visit again, but dang it, couldn't the woman pick a better time? As she lamented, Chris continued speaking. "You go get dressed."

Silva nodded as she raced into their bedroom and began scouring through her drawers for panties, a bra, and some clothes.

Embarrassing.   Embarrassing.   Embarrassing. Embarrassing. This was so embarrassing. She couldn't believe Kuro had just randomly shown up out of the blue like this. Of course, she was happy to see her friend. Of course she was. But still... still... why did it have to be right now? Silva had been hoping to show off to Chris, so he would lose himself to lust and take her in the kitchen. Now her dreams were completely dashed! Crushed before they even started!

After sliding her panties up her hips and hooking the front clasp of her bra, Silva put on a pair of pink pajama pants with a hole in the back for her tail and a white shirt. Imprinted on the shirt was the face of a green-haired young man who looked a little girlish. Below the face were the words *"Become the warrior."* Once she was dressed, the still embarrassed Silva wandered out of the bedroom.

Chris had already set the table. Two plates sat on a pair of placemats. There were napkins, forks, and steak knives out as well. The salad bowl was sitting between the plates, and Chris had already placed both steaks on their respective plates and salads. When she entered the living room, he looked up and smiled.

"It looks like we might need an extra steak for Kuro," he said to her. "Do we have anymore?"

Silva frowned just a little as she glanced at Kuro, sitting over on the couch and staring at her, and tried to remember if they had anymore steak.

"I think... these were the only steaks we had," Silva admitted after a moment. They only shopped for two and didn't buy extra food on the off chance that they might have guests. In fact, guests were pretty much non-existent. Kuro had been the only person who came over and she had stopped after she watched them have sex that one time.

"In that case, I'll whip up something really simple and Kuro can have my steak," Chris said after a bit of thinking.

Silva's ears and tail drooped. "That steak was meant for you, though..."

She had worked really hard to make this delicious steak for Chris. One of the greatest joys she had right now was hearing Chris call her food delicious. The only thing that would have been better was if Chris's clothes randomly exploded off his body after he a bite of her cooking, but she knew stuff like that only happened in anime.

Chris chuckled as he walked over to her, the pleasant sound tickling her ears and causing them to twitch. He placed a hand under her chin and lifted her head. Silva caught a glimpse of his bright eyes before he leaned in and pressed their lips together. His kiss was searing. Silva's knees grew weak from the passion in his kiss, so much so that she would have fallen backward if he hadn't wrapped his arms around her waist.

"Thank you," he said. "I really appreciate you cooking for me. To be honest, I don't like the idea of giving my food to someone else, but we have to be proper hosts."

"I... I know that," Silva muttered. If she'd had an extra steak, she would have gladly cooked another for Kuro. She wanted Kuro to try her food too, especially since Kuro hadn't been around for a few days. Her cooking had grown by leaps and bounds.

"You know... you were awfully sexy in that apron," Chris said suddenly.

"R-really?" Silva perked up.

"Mmhmm." Chris smiled and pressed their foreheads together. "So tonight... would you mind wearing it again?"

"I-I can do that," Silva said, her imagination quickly spinning out of control. She didn't think they would be doing it in the kitchen like she originally planned, but even so, the idea of having sex while wearing nothing but an apron still appealed to her.

"Okay. Tonight then," Chris confirmed.

"Tonight," Silva said.

Chris removed his arms from her waist and wandered into the kitchen, leaving Silva slightly dazed and standing in the living room. Kuro, still seated on the couch, was looking at her with an oddly embarrassed expression.

"You… have become really perverted, haven't you?" she asked.

"Meow?" Silva blinked as she came back to herself, then looked at Kuro. "W-what do you mean? I'm not perverted…" She looked away. "It's completely natural to want to have sex with the person you love."

"I guess…"

Kuro didn't look convinced, but she at least didn't say anything more.

Since Chris had kindly given up his steak for Kuro, the dark-skinned catgirl moved over to the table and sat down in the spot normally reserved for him. Silva felt a little awkward having someone who wasn't Chris sitting across from her. Even so, she couldn't help but stare in anticipation at Kuro as the other catgirl cut a slice of steak off and placed it in her mouth. She held her breath without even realizing it.

"This is... really good," Kuro said, surprised. She cut another slice of steak and chewed on it. Her eyes widened. "This is delicious!"

Silva released the breath she'd been holding and smiled. "I'm glad you like it."

"Now I'm jealous," Kuro admitted. "Does Chris get to eat like this everyday?"

"I don't always make steak if that's what you mean," Silva said. "But I like cooking, so I usually cook dinner now. The only days I don't cook dinner are when Chris doesn't have school. He said it's important that he also helps out around the house."

She and Chris had done their best to divide any and all housework between each other. Silva was in charge of cleaning the bedroom and doing the laundry, while Chris cleaned the living room, bathroom, kitchen, and took out the trash. Silva also did most of the cooking since Chris almost always came home late, but he would clean the dishes. The only day he cooked was Sunday when he didn't have school or kickboxing.

"Now I'm really jealous," Kuro admitted.

"As you should be," Chris said as he came in with a plate of chicken risotto and sat down. It was leftovers from the previous night. He must have heated it up in the microwave.

"Silva is an amazing cook. She's already way better than I am."

Silva blushed at the compliment while Kuro grumbled under her breath. After the initial grumbling was out of the way, the much taller and more muscular catgirl began eating with a tad more force, as if her jealousy had become evident in the way she tore into her steak like a rabid animal.

Dinner was mostly silent after their initial conversation. Once everyone finished eating, Chris took their plates away, put them in the dishwasher, and washed the pan and cutting board Silva had used to cook with. Silva and Kuro, meanwhile, went over to the couch. Chris joined them a few minutes later.

"Okay," Chris began, "Silva, I'm sure you're wondering why Kuro is here. She actually came to the kickboxing center this afternoon. It seems she has something she wants our help with."

Silva looked at Kuro, who suddenly seemed oddly... nervous? No, it was more like she was embarrassed. The woman sat there, twiddling her thumbs and looking at everything except them. However, she eventually coughed into her hand and began speaking.

"So... you two know how me and the other catgirls are living in that orphanage, and you also know that the orphanage currently has some problems with that loan shark

Sister Ann went through to get a loan so she could pay off her bills, right?" When Chris and Silva nodded, she continued. "Well, Lafaard has given her a due date. Sister Ann has to somehow get $125,000 by April 16th. If she can't, then he will seize the orphanage and the church attached to it."

Chris didn't know how legal this Calvin Lafaard's actions were, but he assumed all this information had been written into the contract using legal loopholes that only someone who specialized in understanding legal jargon would figure out. Sister Ann would obviously not have understood and probably just signed the contract out of desperation.

"So, what do you want from us, exactly?" asked Chris.

"I know this is a lot to ask, but can you please help us somehow raise enough money to pay off our debt?"

As she made this request, Kuro twisted her body on the couch and bowed to Chris and Silva, who could do nothing more than stare at her.

***

Because Kuro's request wasn't something Chris could just agree to on the spot, he asked Kuro if she could stay the night. He promised to give her an answer tomorrow morning. The woman had agreed.

Since they didn't have anywhere else for her to sleep, Chris had gotten out several blankets and extra pillows for Kuro, who had taken the couch in the living room. She didn't seem to mind. Kuro had even mentioned how this couch was softer than the bed she slept on at the orphanage, though all that did was make Chris feel sympathy for her and the other catgirls.

At present, Chris was sitting on the bed, dressed in just his boxer shorts, thinking about Kuro's situation.

He did want to help. Chris did not approve of what was happening to that orphanage. More than that, Kuro and the others were victims of the same man who had abused Silva. If he could do something to help them out, then he wanted to do it. The problem was he didn't know what he could do to help. Was there anything that a regular college student like him could accomplish?

Thoughts like that were driven from his mind when Silva suddenly walked into the bedroom from the bathroom.

She was wearing the apron again.

Nothing but the apron.

As the catgirl walked over to the bed with small, delicate steps, the hem of her apron shifted, revealing more of her milky thighs. The apron wrapped around her body prevented him from seeing too much. Even so, he could see her collarbone, slender shoulders, and elegant neck. In some ways, knowing that Silva was not wearing anything underneath that apron but not being able to see her was more erotic than if she had been completely nude. The knowledge alone was enough to make his mouth go dry.

"W-what do you think?" asked Silva, stuttering just a bit.

"I think… I really want you right now," Chris admitted as he took a deep breath. "Seeing you wearing something like this is a huge turn on."

"I'm so glad you like it." Silva placed a hand against her chest and clutching her apron in relief.

Chris smiled as he climbed off the bed and walked over to Silva, taking the slender catgirl into his arms and leaning down to claim those sweet lips. She tasted of mint and baking soda. Silva used a type of toothpaste made specifically for catgirls, which had a similar flavor to the Arm & Hammer toothpaste that Chris used. However, mixed within the taste of toothpaste was Silva's unique flavor, which he could never get enough of.

As he pushed his tongue into Silva's mouth, Chris reached down and grabbed a handful of her rear end, grasping, squeezing, and kneading her small bottom like a baker kneaded dough. His finger sank into her pliant flesh. While her ass was small, it had a perfectly round shape and was soft like marshmallows.

A soft mewling sound escaped Silva's lips as her thighs and butt cheeks clenched in his hands. Her arms went around his back. She pulled herself close, pressing her breasts into his chest, which he could feel through the apron. After several moments of being lost in her mouth, Chris pulled back.

"S-Silva... could you lean over the bed, please?"

At his request, Silva walked to the foot of the bed, placed her hands against the mattress, and leaned over. This had the effect of pushing her ass out. Her tail was standing straight up. As he stared at her deliciously tight rump, he also had a great glimpse of her pussy. She was already aroused. Her glistening nether lips were calling to him.

"Like this?" Silva asked, turning her head to glance at him. A blush lit up her cheeks. They had never done something like this before, so she must have been feeling a tad embarrassed.

"Mmm. Just like that," Chris replied as he knelt on the floor behind her.

Silva bit her lip as Chris reached out and spread her ass cheeks apart. Her cute little butthole had a healthy pink color. If he was giving her a checkup, he would have said her asshole was perfectly healthy. That actually gave him a good idea. Maybe they should play doctor some time. He knew there were stores that specialized in selling fetish cosplay. It shouldn't be too hard to find a patience smock and sexy doctor outfit. Maybe they would have a good codpiece…

"C-Chris… it's a little embarrassing with you just staring at me like that," Silva murmured, her thighs trembling as a light sweat broke out on her skin.

"Sorry," he apologized. "I was just admiring the moon tonight."

"The moon? But you're not even near a windOOOWW! MREOW!"

Silva's confused words were completely stolen from her when Chris leaned forward and buried his face in her snatch.

***

"MREOW!"

Kuro jerked up, startled awake by the loud and erotic moaning that echoed through the walls. She looked around. Panic spread through her for a second, causing her heart to race, before she realized where she was. This wasn't Markus Flint's prison. This wasn't the orphanage. This was Chris Redford's apartment.

"S-so good! Mreow! Meow!"

As the wanton moans continued to echo all around her, Kuro finally realized what was going on. Blood rushed to her cheeks as Silva's moaning and mewling reached her through the walls.

"Honestly... those two... couldn't they at least have the decency not to have sex while I'm here?" she muttered bitterly before laying down down and trying to go to sleep.

"C-Chris! Your tongue! Your tongue is—mreow!—it's devouring me! Oh! I! Meow! I feel like I'm losing my mind!"

Yet there was absolutely no way Kuro could sleep now. She was wide awake. Wide awake and horny as fuck.

Before Kuro even realized what she was doing, her hand slid down her pants and sought out her pussy. She moaned softly as she pressed a finger against her lips and began rubbing it. Biting her lip, she felt a jolt race through her body as she slid her finger along her labia. Her breathing picked up, growing heavier, headier.

As Silva's cries continued to echo from her, Kuro reached out with her other hand and grabbed her breasts through her shirt. She wasn't wearing a bra at the moment. Her nipple quickly stiffened as she pinched it through the fabric of her shirt. The feeling sent electricity racing through her body, causing the muscles in her thighs and calves to tighten. Even her toes spasmed a little.

But it wasn't enough.

She couldn't cum.

An internal battle waged within her mind before she got up from the couch and made her way to Chris and Silva's bedroom, opened the door a crack, and peered inside. What she saw made her remember the night she had barged in on the two while they were having sex. They normally stopped right before doing the deed, but that time she had caught them as they were fucking, and they hadn't stopped.

It had been one of the hottest things she had ever seen.

However, what she saw now topped that.

Silva was bending over the bed, her legs spread wide, back arched as Chris knelt before her, eating out the catgirl's pussy. Kuro couldn't see what he was doing. However, she knew his face was buried in her snatch, lapping up Silva's juices and pressing his tongue into her folds. Her fellow catgirl's breathing was ragged as if she'd been running a marathon. Loud "Mreows!" echoed from her mouth, which was wide open and had drool leaking from it. Silva's tail trembled as it remained sticking straight up in the air.

Kuro bit her lip as she watched them, inserting a finger into her sopping wet cunt. She curled her finger to reach that sweet spot inside of her and rubbed furiously, feeling the way her walls convulsed around her finger. Her juices dripped onto her hand and began staining her pants.

"MREOOOOWWW!"

As she watched, Silva threw her head back and released a cry so erotic that Kuro almost orgasmed on the spot. The smaller catgirl shuddered for several seconds as every muscle in her body seemed to tighten. Then she slumped forward, her torso falling onto the bed while her ass and legs hung off.

Chris stood up and removed his boxers. Once he did, Kuro felt a moan threaten to escape her lips as his cock sprang free.

She was no blushing virgin. While Kuro was picky about her men, she'd been with several back when she was in the military. There were times when her mating season hit and no amount of sex toys or fingers could give her what she needed. She would sometimes take the pill that quelled her mating period. But sometimes she just needed a good fucking.

Back when she was on deployment, she would occasionally head to an international breeders branch and find a man who suited her tastes to fuck. She preferred rugged men. Guys with defined, hard muscles that she could lick and savor. Kuro had enjoyed finding those men among the breeders and dominating them.

Chris fit her preference perfectly, with his broad shoulders, well-defined back, six-pack abs, and muscular ass and thighs. However, it was his dick that was really getting her turned on right now. She was no good judge in size, but Chris was clearly bigger than most of the breeders she'd slept with. His cock was large and throbbing. There were several veins running along its surface.

For just a moment, Kuro wondered what it would be like to have that thing shoved up her pussy. She pictured herself pushing Chris down like she'd done during their spar, mounting him, and shoving that hot, throbbing WMD into her cunt. Her body shuddered as the imagery invoked a greater response in her. Needing to get that release more than ever now, Kuro worked out her clit from beneath its hood and pinched it between her thumb and index finger.

At that exact moment, Chris grabbed Silva's hips, lined his cock up with her entrance, and pushed himself inside of her. Silva, who looked like she was unconscious, suddenly arched her spine and released another loud moan as he bottomed out.

"Ugh... Chris... mreow... your dick... it's filling me up!"

"And your pussy is so tight I can barely move," Chris grunted as he pulled his hips back, then pushed them forward. He moved at a slow pace, working his movements into a rhythm that caused Silva to raise her hips and grind herself against him every time he pushed his cock inside of her.

From her position kneeling by the door, Kuro could see the way Chris's balls were slapping against Silva's ass. As he continued screwing her, Chris leaned forward, pressed his chest to Silva's back as he reached around, slipped his hands into her apron, and grabbed her tits.

"I love you so much, Silva," he said. His voice was a heavy growl. The guttural, primal sound caused Kuro to leak more juices around her fingers. She bit her lip to stop herself from moaning. "I love this cute little ass, these perky tits, that beautiful pussy... I love how adorable you are when you cook, the way your cute nose wiggles when you're thinking hard about something. I love everything about you!"

Silva's moaning was growing in frequency and intensity as Chris spoke to her. The loving words combined with his actions seemed to cause Silva's entire body to grow weak. At the same time, her love juices were dripping down her legs, mixing with her sweat. They stained the floor.

"T-then show me! Please! C-cum! Cum now! I can't— mreow! I can't take it anymore!"

Kuro gritted her teeth as the heat within her loins surged. Jolts of pleasure shot through her spine as she continued playing with her clit, pinching it, rubbing it, pressing her finger against it. Her pace increased in time with Silva's moaning. The other catgirl's lewd, wanton moans spurred her on, making her actions grow more and more feverish.

A tight pressure caused her abdomen and legs to spasm. Kuro knew her end was close. Wanting—no, *needing*—that release, Kuro pinched her clit hard.

"MREOWW!!"

As she came, her pussy flooding with her orgasm, Silva released a loud cry that fortunately overpowered Kuro's gasping moan.

The silver-haired catgirl would have fallen forward. However, she was trapped within Chris's embrace as he shot his load inside of her. His hips jerked several times, his ass cheeks clenching. Several seconds passed. Then his flaccid dick slid out of her pussy, his seed spilling from her lips and dripping down her legs.

Silva was finished. The catgirl didn't even have the strength to hold herself up, so Chris scooped her into his arms and walked toward the head of the bed. He set her down, then climbed in himself. Just as he was about to pull the covers over them, he glanced at the door, and Kuro, out of fear, quickly bolted away before he could see her.

She made her way back to the couch, threw the covers over herself, and closed her eyes. However, no matter how hard she tried, sleep would not come.

"Fuck. I'm still so horny," she whispered in discontent.

chapter 6

Chris woke up early in the morning, took a shower, and began making breakfast. Silva was still fast asleep, and Kuro was conked out on the couch. When he last saw her, the woman had been sleeping with her face buried in her pillow, her left leg and arm hanging off the couch, and her tail swishing around like she was having a dream.

He let her sleep and made his way into the kitchen, where he cooked up a simple breakfast of scrambled eggs with cheese, toast with butter, and a glass of orange juice for him and milk for SIlva and Kuro. He didn't know if Kuro liked milk.

It was odd. Popular culture about catgirls like ads and commercials would often depict catgirls drinking milk. Catgirls, in general, loved the taste of milk because of its fat content. The fatty cream of milk was something that a catgirl's tastebuds generally craved, though not always, and because of this love for the stuff, it wasn't unusual to see a cute or sexy catgirl being used on an ad for milk.

However, the truth was that milk wasn't exactly good for a catgirl to drink. It was fine when they were young. When catgirls were still nursing, milk would be an important source of nutrients. What's more, catgirl babies were capable of producing the enzyme known as lactase in their gut, which was needed to digest lactose, the complex sugar found in milk, into its simplest components: galactose and glucose.

Of course, like cats, it was important not to feed them cow's milk when they were young. Cow's milk didn't have the component nutrients found in a catgirl mother's breast milk. Replacing one with the other was likely to cause upset stomachs and other gut related issues. Humans who became the guardian of catgirls generally bought replacement products made specifically for catgirl consumption.

As catgirls got older, their bodies became more in line with regular humans, so it was possible for them to drink and digest cow's milk, but that didn't necessarily make it healthy. There were problems with catgirls potentially becoming addicted to cow's milk if they drank too much, which could lead to health issues like obesity, heart related problems, and stomach issues.

That was why Chris only kept a small carton for Silva. He didn't want her to overdrink. One glass in the morning was enough.

Maybe it was the scent of the food, but loud sniffing echoed from the living room as Kuro, her long dark hair in complete disarray, sat up and stumbled off the couch. She made her way into the kitchen where he was cooking. She stopped and stood in the doorway, staring at him with this unfathomable expression, like she couldn't understand what he was doing there.

"Good morning," Chris said. "Breakfast will be ready in a moment, so why don't you wake up Silva and take a seat at the table."

Kuro blinked several times. She still didn't seem fully cognizant, but she nodded anyway and shambled off to this bedroom. While she was waking up Silva, Chris set out three plates on the table. Each plate had a good portion of eggs and two pieces of toast. He also brought out the milk. By the time he was finished setting everything up, a sleepy Silva and a more awake than before Kuro sat down.

"Smells... goooooooddd... meow..." Silva yawned, even as she leaned in to smell the food. There was a sleepy smile on her face that put Chris at ease.

"Dig in, you two," Chris said. "And let me know if you want seconds. We've got a bit more left."

"Kay," Silva said, yawning again as she grabbed her fork and began eating.

"Thank you for the food," Kuro said as she also began eating.

Breakfast was eaten in silence. None of them were completely awake yet. However, as they ate, Chris knew he needed to speak with Kuro before leaving for school.

"I've been thinking about your situation," he said to the catgirl, who perked up and focused on her bright eyes on him. "On my own, there isn't much that I can do. I don't have any clout, so anything I did wouldn't amount to much." Just as Kuro's shoulders began slumping, Chris smiled and continued. "However, I do have a friend in my class whose mother is an important figure that advocates catgirl rights. I'm sure if I ask her, she can help us."

Kuro needed several moments to think about this and understand what he meant. During that time, Silva finished her food and polished off her glass of milk. The silver-haired catgirl sat back with a content sigh and smacked her lips before focusing on Kuro, whose dimmed eyes slowly brightened.

"Then does that mean…" she began before trailing off.

Chris nodded. "It means I'll do what I can to help you."

***

Chris left soon after he finished breakfast. He had school to attend, so he couldn't afford to stay long. Since he cooked breakfast and needed to leave quickly after eating, Silva decided to clean the table, but once that was done, she and Kuro sat on the couch and she turned on the TV. There weren't any good cooking shows, so she flipped on Netflix and turned on *The Seven Deadly Sins*.

Outside of watching Chef Ramsay, that was her favorite show right now.

She was on season 2.

"Chris…" Kuro began as the opening theme song began playing. "He's a really good guy, isn't he?"

"Chris is a great person," Silva agreed. She glanced at Kuro out of the corner of her eye. The other catgirl wasn't watching the anime but staring at her. She turned back to the TV. "When he first found me after I had run away from Markus, he treated my injuries, fed me good food, and looked after me as I sorted through my issues. He never pushed me

for anything and always gave me a handed when I needed it."
A smile blossomed unbidden on her face. "That's why I fell in
love with him."

"It has nothing to do with his dick?" asked Kuro.

"His dick came later," Silva admitted before freezing.
She glanced at Kuro, who also seemed to realize what she had
just said.

"Ah..." The dark-skinned woman's throat seemed to
close up as she raised her hands in the air like she was
warding Silva off. "Please forget I said anything."

Silva didn't say anything, but she didn't really have to.
She understood that Kuro had watched them last night from
the other catgirl's words alone.

To be fair, they hadn't been quiet, and she had known
Kuro was on the other side of the living room. Part of her
embarrassment last night stemmed from this fact. However,
while the idea of her friend hearing what she was doing
embarrassed her, it had also added extra stimulation to her
senses. Knowing Kuro could hear what they had been doing,
wondering if the woman would peek on her and Chris while
they had sex, imagining her doing it... these thoughts had
aroused her as much as they ashamed her.

Maybe she really was becoming a pervert.

"Do you like Chris?" Silva suddenly asked.

"Huh?" Kuro looked startled by the question, but she settled down a few seconds later, rubbing her thighs together as she tried to answer. "Well... I mean, I don't know him that well, but he seems like a nice person. Er, uh... I guess you could say I like what I know about him so far?"

Silva nodded. "Do you like him enough to become his catpanion?"

"Excuse me?" Kuro asked.

"Do you want to be—"

"I heard you the first time." Kuro raised a hand to stop Silva from repeating herself. "Sorry, I was just shocked you'd ask me that."

"Why are you shocked?" asked Silva, tilting her head.

"No particular reason, I guess. It just came so suddenly, you know?" Kuro crossed her arms defensively.

"I guess so." Silva paused. "So... do you?"

"Ha... I don't know." Kuro ran a hand down her face. Her hands were much bigger than Silva's. They were even bigger than Chris's. "Like I said, he's a good guy, I can see why you love him, and I'll admit I'm attracted to him... but I don't know if I want to be his catpanion. I mean, I've never been somebody's catpanion before, and I'm... well, I'm not exactly cute and innocent like you are."

Silva didn't know what being cute and innocent had to do with being someone's catpanion, but she knew that everyone had different ideas about the matter. She had only just learned about catpanions herself a little while ago, back when she and Chris had dinner with Tanner and his catpanion, Akari.

"Okay. Well, let me know if you do," Silva said. "I've been thinking about this, and I think it would be nice if Chris had another catpanion." She lifted her feet onto the couch and hugged her knees to her chest as a small smile crossed her face. "I like living with Chris, but it gets kind of lonely when he's off by himself. It would be nice if I had someone else living with me."

Silva would admit her reasons for wanting Kuro to be Chris's catpanion was entirely selfish. She wanted someone else to live with her, so when Chris was out, she wouldn't be so lonely. Kuro was her best friend. She was also the person who saved Silva from Markus. It would be comforting to her if this catgirl also became Chris's catpanion.

Kuro stared at her for a few seconds, then gave her a wan smile.

"I think you just want to add me to your nightly activities."

"T-that isn't it!" Silva denied furiously as heat rose to her cheeks.

"Pervert," Kuro whispered with a grin.

"Mreow! I am not a pervert!" Silva cried out.

***

Chris stepped off the bus, his backpack slamming against his back as he fast-walked through the San Diego State University's campus. He ignored most of the people who were walking around him. There were a lot. A group of athletes walked past him, chatting about some girls they met at a party. A pair of girls looked at him as he walked by and smiled. He smiled back, then grimaced when they walked past, giggling to themselves.

There weren't many catgirls present, but it had only been recently that catgirls had been allowed to attend college.

And it was the daughter of the woman who made this possible that he wanted to speak with.

It was Tuesday today, which meant he was taking Catgirl Biology, a class that he shared with Anastasia Pierce. As he entered the lecture hall, his eyes swept around the interior. He didn't see Anastasia anywhere. Only a handful of people were currently sitting at their desks. Chris didn't let this bother him since she normally showed up later than he did. He walked up to where he normally sat, set his backpack on the ground, and sat down.

Just as he suspected, Anastasia did come into the classroom several minutes after him. Sadly, she did not sit next to him like she used to. She instead sat next to a pair of girls, who she began chatting with, which caused him to lean back in his chair and sigh.

It looked like she was either angry with him or no longer interested in being his friend. He wasn't sure he could blame her. He *did* turn her down, after all. It was never easy confessing your feelings to someone, and it was even harder getting shot down after you did so. Chris understood how that felt.

But now he was in a bind. He really needed to speak with her. She was literally the only person who could help him.

Should he go up and speak to her despite how she probably didn't want to see him right now, or should he wait? It was currently February 14th, which meant he had about one month before Sister Ann's deadline came up. That did give him a lot of leeway in terms of time. However, this was also a double-edged sword. If he thought to himself, *"This can wait because I still have time,"* it could make him complacent. He would never forgive himself if that resulted in Sister Ann being unable to pay off her debt in time for the deadline.

Yet before he could stand up, walk down, and ask Anastasia if he could speak with her after class, the door opened and in walked Professor Shinomiya. The little half-Asian woman walked up to the podium, dressed in her traditional Gothic lolita style outfit and carrying a water bottle and her purse. She set everything down on the table next to the podium and turned to face the class.

"Today, we're going to be learning about bone fractures and the specific steps necessary to heal them. You might think it's the same with catgirls as it is for humans, but there are several differences you need to be aware of. This knowledge will not only be on your next test, but it is important information for the class you will be taking next year, which will involve applying everything you have learned this year into real life practice." Professor Shinomiya paused as her eyes scanned the students before stopping on Chris. "Except you, Chris. The Dean wants to speak with you, so head over to his office."

"Right now?" Chris asked with a frown.

"Right now," Professor Shinomiya confirmed.

Chris furrowed his brow as he glanced at Anastasia, who was specifically not looking at him, then stood up with a sigh and made his way down the stairs. He exited the class, cut across the campus, and walked toward the Dean's office. On the way, he tried to figure out why the Dean would call him. He'd never even spoken to the Dean before in his life.

As he entered the building with the Dean's office, he found himself standing in a small waiting room. A few chairs were pressed against one wall. The other wall had a desk, behind which a relatively large lady sat. She had short brown hair and was wearing pants and a collared shirt. No one aside from this lady was inside the room.

"Excuse me," he said. "My name is Chris Redford. I was called in to see the Dean?"

The woman looked up at him, eyes roaming across his physique, and sighed. "Another one, huh? Well, just sit right over there. The Dean is currently meeting with another student right now."

Another one? Chris wondered what she meant by that, but he didn't say anything as he sat down.

While he was sitting down, Chris decided to text Anastasia. He knew she was in class, so he didn't expect her to respond right away, but he at least wanted to let her know he needed to speak with her.

He got a response faster than he expected.

"I'm not sure I want to talk to you right now."

He frowned, fingers flashing against the keyboard, then hit send. He got another message.

"I'm not upset, but I'm also not really keen on seeing the guy who shot me down days after it happened."

His frowned deepened as he tried to think of what he should say. He really did understand why she might not want to see him, but he also really needed to speak with her. Chris decided to go with honesty as he typed on the keyboard again. He didn't receive a response for several minutes.

"Okay. If you really need help and think I'm the only one who can do it, meet me after class ends. I'll be waiting by the large tree next to the Starbucks we had coffee at the other day."

In other words, she would be waiting by the place where he turned her down. Chris wasn't sure how he felt about that. However, he thanked her before the door to the Dean's office opened and someone walked out. When he looked up, Chris felt his stomach suddenly drop.

The person who had walked out from the Dean's office was Jason Barker.

Jason Barker didn't say anything to him as he walked out of the office, though he did glance in Chris's direction. However, he didn't need to say anything. Chris already had a good guess as to what he had been called in for.

"Chris Redford," the secretary called. "The Dean will see you now."

Chris stood up and entered the Dean's office. He gazed at the pictures hanging from the walls, at the glass case upon which several trophies sat proudly on display, and then at the large desk. Behind the desk was another wall with a lot of sports memorabilia celebrating the long and outstanding sports history of this university. Of course, sitting behind the desk was also the Dean.

The Dean was a thin man. His graying hair and mustache lent him a somewhat rustic look. He made Chris think of a retired cowboy. However, his crisp suit, which looked like it cost more than most people's annual salary, did not compliment this retired cowboy appearance. He probably would have looked more natural if he wore a trench coat and leather chaps.

"Mr. Redford, take a seat," the Dean said. He had a southern or maybe Texan accent. It was hard to tell. Chris had never been good with accents.

"Yes, sir."

Chris took a seat as the Dean clasped his hands and placed them on the desk, dark eyes peering at him from behind wireframe glasses. The chair wasn't exactly comfortable. It was hard and forced him to sit with his back straight. He was sure these chairs were designed this way to make the Dean feel more powerful than the people speaking with him.

"Do you know why I called you here?" the Dean asked.

"Maybe," Chris began, carefully avoiding the man's gaze.

"It has to do with a fight that broke out several days ago," the Dean said. Chris tried really hard not to wince, but he wasn't sure he succeeded. "I know you were involved in that fight. Now, I've spoken with everyone else about this incident except you, so now I'm talking to you. I want you to tell me what happened."

Nodding as he realized there was no way for him to get out of this, Chris did his best to explain what had happened, how he'd stumbled across Jason protecting a catgirl from three jocks, how the jocks had ganged up on Jason, and how he had decided to intervene. The Dean, to his credit, did not react with surprise or even stop him to ask questions. When Chris was finished, the man nodded.

"That matches the story told by Mr. Barker and Ms. Satella," the Dean said. "The three members of our basketball team told it very differently, saying you jumped them while they were just trying to speak with Ms. Satella."

Ms. Satella must have been the catgirl who he saved. Chris had never bothered asking for her name.

"And which side do you believe?" he asked.

"Who I believe doesn't really matter." The chair creaked as the Dean leaned back, the leather conforming to him. "We don't tolerate violence at school, so regardless of who was at fault, all parties have to be punished." He paused, then sighed. "That said, I am more inclined to believe you, Mr. Barker, and Ms. Satella. Those three have been reported several times for misconduct against a female student. They've been given one month suspension and have been expelled from the basketball team. You and Mr. Barker will be receiving a two-week suspension."

Chris wanted to protest his suspension when all he was doing was helping out someone who'd been outnumbered, but he also realized he didn't actually have any room to stand on. This wasn't a case of self-defense. He could have walked away. He didn't because his morals wouldn't let him, but ultimately, the fight that happened was one he could have avoided.

He also knew that arguing would just make his situation worse.

"I understand," Chris said.

"If you understand, then make sure this doesn't happen again," the Dean said.

"Yes, sir."

Without so much as a sigh, Chris stood up and left the Dean's office. He paid the secretary no mind as she typed something on her keyboard. Leaving the office, he glanced at his clock, saw that Catgirl Biology still had two hours left, and decided to grab a bite to eat before heading over to the tree in front of the Starbucks.

***

Chris stood before the giant oak tree located in the center of a small grassy field surrounded by pavement. A few yards in front of him was the building which the Starbucks was attached to. People of various shapes and sizes, some big and some small, some pudgy and some thin, walked through the glass door. Windows along the building allowed him to see the people who were sitting inside, sipping hot mugs of coffee or a latte. Some typed on computers. Other read a book.

There was still some time before he had to meet with Anastasia. He used that time to try and figure out what he was going to tell her. Should he apologize? No. That was a stupid idea since he didn't actually have anything to apologize for. He turned her down, yes, but it wasn't like that was something he shouldn't have done. If anything, telling her straight out that he was already involved with someone was the proper response.

"Alex? Sorry for being a bit late. I had to speak with Professor Shinomiya after class."

"It's no trouble," Alex said as he continued to think. If not an apology, then maybe what he should do was bow and beg her to help him. He'd once heard that a traditional Japanese bow, the kind where a man got down on his hands and knees, face pressed to the ground, was the proper way to ask for a favor... but that was only in anime.

That was no good either.

"So, what did you want to talk about?"

Chris rubbed his jaw and thought hard. What should he say? What should he do? How could he convince Anastasia to help him? He didn't know. Did that mean he would have to wing it?

"Hey! Are you listening to me?!"

"Huh?" Chris looked up, startled, his eyes widening as a pair of gorgeous blues appeared before him. Anastasia's eyes were narrowed with annoyance, her face framed by locks of blonde hair. "I'm sorry. I hadn't realized you were here yet."

Her eyes narrowed further. "What were you thinking so hard about that you didn't even realize I was here?"

He rubbed the back of his head. "I was thinking about what I should say to you."

This admittance took her aback, narrowed eyes slowly growing wide as she reached out and grabbed her left arm with her right hand. She seemed to consider him for a moment before nodding.

"I guess that's an acceptable reason. However, as both an apology and in exchange for me hearing you out, you are going to buy me a coffee and something to eat," she said.

It was a fair deal, one that Chris didn't have a problem with.

They went into the Starbucks, and after waiting in line for several minutes, Anastasia ordered a venti macchiato and a blueberry oat cake. Chris paid for it.

After she had her order taken and they sat down, Anastasia pinched off a piece of her oat cake and placed it in her mouth. Chris shifted a little as her mouth closed around the cake. Her eyes gazed into his with a look that was both delicate and unyielding, but she also seemed confused.

"Okay," she began with a sigh after swallowing her food. "You mentioned a problem you're having that you think I can solve, so let's hear it."

"Thank you," Chris said softly before he proceeded to let her know about his problem.

It was interesting to watch the way her eyes widened as he explained how he'd gone to an orphanage, discovered Silva's catgirl companions, and found out the orphanage was on the verge of being overtaken by a shady businessman who gave Sister Ann an unfair loan that she could never hope to pay back. However, as he spoke, her expression also turned resigned. She knew why he was asking for her help.

"I am sorry to ask this of you." Chris finished by bowing his head toward her. "After what happened between us, I know you don't have any obligation to help me, and I can even understand why you wouldn't want to help me. But you really are the only person I can turn to for help. Please, I want to help Sister Ann keep her orphanage afloat, but I don't have any political power or influence to do it."

"So, what you really want isn't my help, but my mother's," Anastasia said, her tone flat.

"… Yes."

The scent of her blueberry oat cake tickled Chris's nose as he leaned forward, a slightly sweet scent that mixed with the dough. He ignored it, for the most part, and kept his head bowed.

He felt legitimately bad for asking this of her. Chris knew what he was asking of her, knew that she didn't even really like her mom much less get along with the woman, and he knew damn well that he was asking for something unreasonable. But he still asked. What else could he do?

Anastasia sighed. "You really are too earnest for your own good. It makes it impossible to say 'no' to you." As Chris raised his head, Anastasia massaged the bridge of her nose as she gazed at him with a tired smile. "I'll talk to my mother. I can't promise you anything, but I can at least talk to her."

"Thank you," Chris said. "I really appreciate that you're willing to help me."

"If you really appreciate it, then prove it by buying me a refill," Anastasia said, a smile on her face as she held her empty cup aloft.

Chris laughed and went to get her another macchiato.

chapter 7

Several days passed since Chris was suspended for two-weeks and spoke with Anastasia about Sister Ann's problem. Silva had been ecstatic when he told her about it. In fact, she'd been so excited that the first thing she did was throw herself into his arms and kiss him on the lips. Seeing her so happy made his suspension a bit more bearable, but at the same time, he couldn't be as happy as she was.

About the only silver lining to all this was he got to spend more time with Silva.

On that note, spending more time with Silva was nice. Because staying at home was boring, they ended up traveling around a lot, going to stores, malls, and the movies. Now that she was adjusting more to being around people, Silva didn't jump at every little thing and could appreciate all the sights and sounds that she had missed when she was Markus's prisoner. The sight of her smile, like a flower in full bloom, had been enough to make it feel like a weight had been lifted from his shoulders.

He had informed Professor Shinomiya about what happened as well, and while she expressed surprise that he would jump into a fight, along with surprise that Jason Barker helped a catgirl, she had accepted his reasoning. Of course, she still wouldn't show him preferential treatment. However, she did convince one of the students to lend them their notes so he wouldn't fall behind in class. That much, she had said, was her responsibility as a teacher.

Since he didn't have school, Chris had changed his schedule a bit. He woke up a little later than usual, had breakfast with Silva, and then he and Silva would go outside for several hours and do something, anything. Afterward, they would come back, Chris would spend several hours working on his commissions, and Silva would watch Chef Ramsay.

Then he would head to the kickboxing center.

Sometimes, Kuro would join him and Silva when they went out, but Chris had the distinct feeling she'd been avoiding him lately. He wasn't sure why. Call it a hunch. The few times they had been out, she had walked on Silva's other side, listening to everything Silva said and responding with a smile, but she studiously ignored him.

There had been a few instances when she forgot she was avoiding him for reasons only she could fathom. One time when they had gone to the movies, Silva had gone to the restroom, leaving them alone. He'd made a joke about how he was surprised she hadn't gone with her since women traveled in packs, but Kuro had told him she was a different breed of cat. There had been a smirk on her face. However, the smirk had left moments later when she realized who she was talking to.

She clammed up after that.

That wasn't the only incident. There had been numerous other times when this had happened. It was getting to the point where Chris wanted to sit the catgirl down, ask her what was wrong, and fix whatever problem she had with him. Sadly, there had never been a good time since she was only with him when Silva was present.

"*Pprrrr!* Mreow... that feels sho good!"

At present, Chris was at home, sitting on the couch, and Silva's head was resting in his lap. She was purring, tail swishing back and forth, a blissful expression on her face. A bit of drool was leaking from her lips. It wouldn't have surprised him if hearts suddenly appeared in her eyes.

Chris was cleaning her ears.

Catgirls were a lot like humans in that they were prone to wax build ups. Certain species of catgirl built up more wax than even some humans did. This was why it was important to clean their ears every so often.

Chris was using a seki edge traditional bamboo ear pick. They were handcrafted ear picks that he had gotten from Japan, with curved ends for scooping out wax and made high quality but flexible bamboo. The bamboo was used for its springiness. Not only that, but the bowl shaped spoon made it easy to scoop the wax out, and the bamboo was soft enough that it didn't irritate the ear canals.

There was only one real problem with this whole thing.

A catgirl's ears were sensitive.

Very sensitive.

"Mreow... Chris... ha... ha... I think I'm gonna cum..."

"Please don't," Chris said dryly as he kept a gentle but firm grip on her ear. He applied a slight amount of pressure as he bent down and scooped some wax out. The feeling of the soft bowl gently scraping against the inside of her ear sent Silva into a series of full body shudders. Her breathing increased as did her mewling. As he watched the catgirl, he turned his head toward her shapely legs and saw the way her toes spasmed. It was the same kind of spasms she gave when she was close to orgasming.

Chris had never once considered ear cleaning to be in any way sexy. Not once. It was gross. You scooped the ear pick inside of someone's ear and scraped out this disgusting yellow goop. How in the hell was that sexy? These had been his thoughts for the longest time.

Now he was just confused.

So confused.

"Mreowwwww... *prrrrr*... nya... ha... ha..."

Silva looked so utterly blissful. There was a dopey look on her face, eyes glazed over as her heavy and heady breathing caressed his legs through his pants. Her tail was standing straight up, pointed toward the sky, just another sign of her happiness.

Not only were her moans incredibly erotic, but she was rubbing and scratching his thighs. When she shifted, the fabric of her dress scooted up, revealing more and more of her thighs. Her white thighs with their beautifully unblemished complexion, which he often spent his nights kissing and licking, were showcased in most of their splendor.

So, yeah, despite the fact that he thought scooping ear wax out of someone's ear was gross, Chris couldn't deny his impulse to reach over and stroke her ass or rub her pussy through her panties. He'd even caught himself nearly reaching out to caress her breasts through the dress. Only an iron will stopped him.

"Okay…" He sighed in relief. "Your left ear is done. You can sit up now."

"I don't know if I can… get up…" Silva admitted.

He didn't understand what she meant at first, but then he noticed how her arms were struggling and how her legs couldn't seem to hold her own weight. Even her torso looked like it had turned into gelatin. Chris could only frown as he pushed the catgirl's head back onto his lap and began stroking her hair. He had completely underestimated the power of cleaning her ears.

"Then I guess you can just rest for now."

"M'kay. Thanks, Chris."

"Sure. No problem."

As he and Silva sat there, Chris's phone began ringing. He glared at the thing sitting on the table in front of him. Reaching out as he leaned over, he grabbed the phone, accepted the call, and pressed it to his ear.

"Hello?" he asked.

"Chris? It's Anastasia."

He perked up. "Anastasia. Hey. Is everything okay?"

"Everything is fine. Listen, about your request… I spoke to my mother."

His throat went dry. "What did she say?"

"She's sympathetic to that sister's plight. She told me she is willing to help you guys out, but she needs you to do several things for her first."

"What are they?" asked Chris.

"First, you need to create a Go-Fund Me account for this. She's planning to try and get several people at her convention to send donations through it. Second, she wants you to create a banner for her. I told her about how you do art commissions. She plans on using that banner to attract her followers. She also said you should make a banner to advertise this on social media and other websites."

"I can do all of those."

With his suspension still a week from being over, Chris had nothing but time on his hands right now. He'd already finished all of his current commissions too. That meant he really did have nothing to do for awhile.

"Is there anything else?" he asked.

"There is one more thing…"

The way Anastasia trailed off and the hesitance in her voice made Chris realize whatever she wanted to ask wasn't easy for her. He waited patiently for her to finish whatever she wanted to say. Whatever he'd been expecting, however, what she said next was not it.

"She wants to you and your catpanion to help her out at the convention. She also wants to meet that sister you spoke of

and have her present her case to the people who will be donating money to her cause. If you do all that, she said she would be willing to help you present the Go-Fund Me to the people attending her convention."

Chris felt like he could understand why she'd been reluctant to tell him this. She and her mother didn't get along, and Chris had shot her down when she confessed, and now her mother wanted to have the boy she confessed to—and got rejected by—along with his catpanion to help her with a convention. That had to be hard on her. Yet she was still willing to help him.

His respect for Anastasia rose.

"Please let her know we'll be there. At least, my catpanion and I will. I don't know about the others, but I'll do my best to convince them." He paused. "We don't need to dress up, do we? I don't have any clothes for an event where the rich and famous will be attending."

"Don't worry about that," Anastasia said, and for the first time, he thought he heard a smirk in her voice. *"My mother said she'll pay the cost of your clothing."*

Chris felt a moment of relief, but it quickly left as he wondered why a famous actress and political advocate would go so far just to help him. A shiver ran down his spine. Whatever the reason was, he wasn't sure he would like it.

***

Since he'd finished cleaning Silva's ears, and he didn't have anything better to do, the two of them hopped onto a bus that took them to the orphanage Sister Ann ran. The kids from before were playing out front again. It looked like they were playing a game of tag this time. A few waved at him and Silva as they passed, but most just stared and pointed.

Sister Ann didn't appear to be in her office. He knocked several times and received no answer.

"Maybe she's in the kitchen?" Silva suggested.

Chris nodded. "Let's look for her, or would you like to visit the other catgirls?"

Silva thought about that, nose wiggly cutely. "I think… I'm going to visit my friends."

"In that case, could you also tell them about what Anastasia said? Let them know that none of them have to go to this convention, but tell them about it anyway just in case they would like to help," Chris said.

"I will." Silva flashed him a smile before moving off.

Chris walked down the hall, through the cafeteria, and entered the kitchen. He frowned when he noticed no one was there. Of course, it was after lunch, so it wasn't like he should have expected anyone to be present, but still…

He shook his head.

Since Sister Ann wasn't in the kitchen, Chris went around the orphanage, occasionally bumping into the kids and asking if they knew where Sister Ann was. Most of them said they didn't know; a few giggled. Chris had the oddest feeling that something was happening to the good sister.

He got his answer after several more minutes of wandering. A little girl about five or six years answered his question in a way that only a child could.

"She and Jason are in her bedroom," the girl said matter-of-factly. "They're naked hugging right now. I saw them."

Chris felt his face burn as amusement, shame, and disgust mixed together. He was amused that this girl would say it so blatantly, ashamed to have heard it, and disgusted because, well, he honestly didn't want to know what Sister Ann and Jason got up to on their free time. That said, it was good to know the two of them were in a relationship. At least, he hoped they were in a relationship. He didn't want to imagine a woman of the cloth having a fuck buddy.

Since it looked like the sister was... busy, Chris now realized he didn't have much to do. He could have gone to see Silva and Kuro, but he thought it was important to give them time to talk amongst themselves. Girl talk was an important bonding experience, sort of like how guys did male bonding by ragging on each other.

With nothing to do, Chris decided to wait by Sister Ann's office. Fortunately, it looked like the dear sister and Jason had started having sex quite a bit earlier than he had arrived. She appeared about fifteen minutes after he reached her office again. Her hair was damp, showing she'd just taken a shower. He couldn't see Jason anywhere, but knowing the guy as he did, Chris imagined the hard to deal with young man was still lazing in bed.

"Chris," Sister Ann said in surprise. "I hadn't realized you were here."

"I wanted to speak with you," Chris said. "I thought about calling, but figured this would be a nice opportunity to let Silva see her friends."

Chris wasn't sure "friends" was the right word, but he hesitated to call them companions. They seemed to get along well enough anyway. Kuro, at least, he thought was a friend. She visited enough anyway.

"Okay. Why don't we talk in my office?" Sister Ann suggested.

They entered her office, which was just a small square room with a desk and some chairs. It honestly didn't look like it was originally meant for this purpose. He would have said it looked more like a storage space that had been converted into an office, but he wasn't going to say anything. This orphanage was rundown, and sometimes you had to make do with what you had.

"What did you want to talk about?" asked Sister Ann as she sat behind the desk, which again, wasn't much of a desk. It was a table. There was a file cabinet underneath it that acted as a drawer.

"Kuro told me about your problem," Chris started off with that. Sister Ann stiffened in her seat, but he plowed on before she could say anything. "She said you have until April 16th to pay off your debt or Calvin Lafaard is going to seize this orphanage and the church attached to it. She asked me to help."

"I'm sorry she asked you that," Sister Ann apologized. "No one but her and Jason know about this. The kids know something is up, but I haven't told them anything because… I honestly don't know what to say."

Chris nodded. "I understand this is a difficult situation. In either event, I've decided to lend you a hand."

"You have?" Sister Ann's eyes widened.

"I have," Chris confirmed. "And I've even figured out how to help you."

As Chris outlined his plan to Sister Ann, the woman became more and more surprised, but after the shock settled, a wide smile spread across her face. It must have been a relief to know that her monetary issues might be over... at least for now.

Sister Ann thanked him profusely several times. Chris did his best to wave her gesture off. He wasn't comfortable with how effusive her gratitude was. Actually, having a woman practically falling over herself to thank him was a little disconcerting. Gratitude was one thing, but Sister Ann had nearly shoved her head into the floor as she bowed to him.

He went over to where the catgirls were staying after he spoke with Sister Ann. When he arrived, it was to find seven catgirls sitting around in the small room they'd been allotted, talking and giggling about something. Silva appeared to be the center of attention. However, all that changed the moment they noticed Chris enter the room.

While Chris recognized Kuro by her muscular body and tall physique, the others he didn't really know that well.

The first girl sitting next to Silva was a fairly normal catgirl. She was neither tall nor short, neither busty nor flat. Her modest chest was covered by a plain white shirt and black pants adorned her hips. Light brown hair fell in a short, messy style around her head. He couldn't figure out what race of catgirl she was, but that meant she was probably a mixed breed: A catgirl who was the result of several generations worth of different races mixing.

Another girl next to her was a Munchkin cat, an incredibly short race of catgirls who looked like eternal children. She was eyeing him warily. Her shock of yellow hair was drawn into a tight ponytail behind her head. It was a childish look that suited her appearance. Like the other catgirl, she was wearing clothes that looked like hand-me-downs.

Aside from those two, there was a catgirl with black hair that had a white fringe. Her skin was even paler than Silva's. An albino. He could immediately tell what kind of cat she was by the glowing red eyes peering at him. She had a delicate face. Her small nose was cute, and her rosy lips created a stark contrast with her pale skin.

On the other bed were two more catgirls, a pair of Siamese twins, sitting next to Kuro. They weren't as small as the Munchkin catgirl, but their bodies looked positively tiny beside the larger Kuro. They had pale skin, off-white hair that traveled down their backs in elegant curls, and black ears. Glowing blue eyes stared at him, though not with suspicion. If he had to say what it was, he would have said they were looking at him with curiosity.

"Uh… hey." Chris waved his hand, disconcerted by the intense stares he was being given. "I just came to pick up Silva."

"Are we leaving already?" asked Silva.

Chris nodded. "We have to do some grocery shopping before heading home."

"Oh. Right."

Silva stood up and made her way over to him, waving goodbye to the others with a smile. Chris nodded toward them in goodbye. However, just as he was about to reach for the door, Kuro stopped him.

"Silva told us about your idea, about how you plan to save the orphanage," she said, causing Chris to retract his hand and turn around. "The girls and I were talking about this, and we've decided that we also want to do what we can. We'd like to help. That said, not all of us are well-suited to crowds. Myself, Lin, Lacy, and Elizabeth have agreed to go to this convention with you."

That was actually more people than he'd expected would go with him. He had figured Kuro would go, if only to watch after Silva, but he hadn't expected any of the others to come with as well. However, Chris was nothing if not adaptable. If they said they could attend, then he would welcome their help.

***

Once they left the orphanage, Chris and Silva took another bus that brought them close to Memorial Park. However, they didn't head straight home. Their fridge was running on empty, so they needed to pick up some food from the grocery store.

Silva hummed as they walked through the aisles, checking prices and looking at ingredients. She'd become quite the penny pincher. That was his influence. Chris lived frugally since he was currently living mostly off student loans. His commissions earned him a decent check, but they were sporadic at best and not something he could rely on for stable income.

"What are you thinking of making tonight?" Chris asked.

"I want to try making beef wellington," Silva replied as she studied the filet mignon.

Beef wellington was a traditional British dish that consisted of a seared filet mignon smothered in a whole-grain mustard and wrapped in layers of salty prosciutto, an herbed crape, duxelles, and puff pastry. The whole package was baked until the crust crisped up and the meat reached a medium-rare cook.

It was a lot more sophisticated than anything Silva had made before. By that, Chris meant there were a lot more steps involved. He didn't know if she could make something like that, but if it was what she wanted to cook, then he would do his best to help.

Beef wellington was made with prime beef fillet. That was easily the hardest thing to find, especially since Silva spent nearly ten minutes trying to judge which one she should get. Prime beef was expensive. She obviously didn't want to spend a lot, but she also knew she couldn't afford to get one of the cheaper ones.

As Silva was looking over the prime beef, Chris noticed three people traveling toward them out of the corner of his eye. Two of them were big, clearly bodyguards, but the third one was the loan shark, Calvin Lafaard. Chris would have wondered what this man was doing here. However, the man's eyes were locked onto his, which made his target clear.

The people in the store cleared the way for this man and his lackeys. Chris eyed them with a calm expression. They were big, and there was no doubt they'd been trained, but having muscles like theirs would slow them down. Their muscles weren't like Tanner's, which were a perfect blend of speed and power. These guys were all power. No speed.

"Can I help you?" asked Chris.

"Hmph. You might be able to," Calvin said with an arrogant snort. "I heard from a little birdy that you plan on helping a certain sister we're both acquainted with."

Chris's frown grew bigger. A little birdy generally referred to a spy, but he couldn't imagine anyone who would spy on Sister Ann... except maybe Jason. However, he didn't want to think badly of Jason since the man seemed an alright sort despite his abrasive personality. That left just one option.

He had planted a recording device somewhere in Sister Ann's room.

"News certainly travels fast," Chris said in a calm, collected voice. This man was a pro. He wouldn't do anything inside of a public area like this. With his shady business practices, he couldn't afford to have a police report filed against him. "What of it?"

"I like that look in your eyes, kid," Calvin said with a smirk. "You've got a good look there. Tell you what. I'm a businessman, and I've been in the business long enough to know that everyone has a price. How much do you want to not attend that convention."

"You want to pay me off so I don't attend the convention?" Chris was flabbergasted. He'd certainly heard of shady businessmen bribing politicians and other people to do something for them, whether that was fudging up their tax records or turning a blind eye to their less than legal business ventures. However, he'd never heard of someone bribing a college student.

It was enough to make him snort.

"Tell you what," Chris began as Silva finally noticed the three guys and came to stand behind him. "I'm a college student. I don't know much about business or anything like that. All I'm doing is attending a convention for a friend.

Nothing suspicious. So why don't you and your men turn around and pretend this conversation never happened."

Calvin narrowed his eyes. "You've got some balls, kid. You're real gutsy. I hope you don't regret this decision of yours." He glanced at Silva, who ducked her head behind Chris when his eyes landed on her. "For your friend's sake if nothing else."

Chris narrowed his eyes, understanding exactly what this man was threatening. He clenched his hands into fists as Calvin turned around and walked off. The two burly men glanced his way, then turned and lumbered behind Calvin, their figures disappearing as they turned a corner.

"Chris, weren't those the guys who came to the orphanage?" Silva asked, peeking her head out from behind him.

"They were," Chris said. "We might have to be on our guard for awhile. Just in case they try something."

"Try something? Like what?" asked Silva, but Chris just shook his head, not answering.

Because, honestly, the thought of what a guy like that might do kind of scared him.

chapter 8

While Sister Ann had an entire month before she needed to pay her loan off, the convention that Anastasia's mother was hosting was happening this weekend. Given how little time there was to prepare, there was no way he could create the Go-Fund Me, artwork for social media advertising, and the banner for Monica Pierce's convention in time. It just wasn't possible.

He needed help.

"Why are we waiting out here again?" asked Kuro.

It was a chilly morning. The brisk air caused goosebumps to appear on Kuro's dark skin, though a lot of that also had to do with her choice of clothing. Decked out in a sleeveless black shirt that showed off her ripped arms, carpenter pants, and boots, it was all too obvious the catgirl would be cold. She wasn't bundled up like Chris and Silva, who had opted to wear sweatpants, long sleeved shirts, and a jacket.

"Because I called someone in to help me get everything done," Chris answered patiently. "She should be arriving any moment now."

They were standing outside at the train station on E Street. Known simply as E Street Station, the small station could hardly be called a station. It was just a couple of benches with a curved half-cylinder roof over it. The tracks lay before them. Meanwhile, across the tracks was a small building for a coffee shop called Cool Down Coffee. Chris had been there once or twice, though never by choice.

E Street Train station was right next to the San Diego Bay, which explained why the scent of salt water drifted to them on the breeze. It also explained why it was so cold. The ocean breeze carried a brisk chill. Across the John J Montgomery Freeway was the San Diego Bay National Wildlife Refuge and Bayside Park.

"I hope this friend of yours arrives soon." Kuro rubbed her arms and shivered.

Chris glanced at her askance. "You should have chosen warmer clothes if you didn't want to be cold."

Kuro scowled. "I didn't know we would be standing outside in the cold when I came over this morning."

Perhaps it was due to the excitement of having something she could do to help Sister Ann, who had taken her and her fellow catgirls in, but Kuro had come to Chris's and Silva's apartment early this morning. When Chris informed her they were traveling to pick someone up, she had decided to tag along.

"Who are we picking up?" asked Silva. "You never did tell me that."

"I guess I didn't." Chris blinked as he realized she was right, but then he shrugged. "Do you remember when I told you about Elsa?" Silva nodded. "She's the one we're picking up here."

"Who is Elsa?" asked Kuro.

"She's the catgirl my parents adopted when I was young." Well, it was more like Chris had forced them to adopt her, but it amounted to the same thing. As he thought about her, a smile worked its way onto his face. "I wonder how she's been doing without me. It's been a little over six months since the last time I saw her."

Chris had seen her when he went back home during the summer break last year and spent almost every waking minute with her. They would stay up late and watch anime, play video games, and go outside during the day. She'd seemed quite lively. However, from the looks his parents had given her, that didn't seem to be how she usually acted.

"Huh. So you have another catpanion besides Silva," Kuro murmured.

But Chris shook his head. "Silva is my only catpanion. Elsa is more like a sister… or something."

"Is she really?" asked Silva.

"Why do I sense doubt in your words?" Chris asked in return.

"No reason," Silva said.

Chris frowned at her, but he caught sight of the next train coming in before he could say anything. He watched eagerly as the bright red train pulled up and slowed to a stop. The doors opened and several people walked out. There weren't many, which was natural considering the early morning, and among them was a girl who caught the attention of every person present.

She was magnificent. Her brilliant blonde hair had been styled into ringlets that fell about her face. Bright blue eyes glowed with a near otherworldly evanescence that made her seem like a creature not of this world. Her ears and tail were as blonde as her hair, but she had white tufts of fur inside of her ears.

A body that drew that gazes of every man—and even some women—revealed itself in all its splendor underneath clothing that was even skimpier than Kuro's. The blue and white skirt didn't even reach down the middle of her thigh. A spirited twirl would reveal her panties. Meanwhile, her shirt only had a single sleeve and resembled a crop top. It featured a high hemline that allowed Chris to glimpse her slender and flat stomach.

Of course, what really drew everyone's gaze was her rack. Sporting breasts almost the same size as Kuro's, her chest bounced with every step she took, and while Chris was sure a part of that was simply because of how flamboyant her walk was, another part was simply due to her breasts massive size. She had mammaries that could have doubled as weapons. Chris had once seen her knock his brother unconscious after accidentally striking him in the face with those things.

"Nya ha ha ha!" The woman stepped in front of him and struck a pose. "I have heard your plight, oh dear Christopher! Heard it and responded to your call! This magical girl has agreed to meet your summons and aid you in your quest! Now be in awe and show proper gratitude! Nya ha ha ha!"

Kuro stared at the catgirl like she was seeing a devil rising from the depths of Hell, but Silva looked impressed. Her eyes sparkled as she clasped her hands under her chin.

"Is that Sakuro Mikage cosplay?!" she asked in shock.

"Nya ha ha ha! You have a discerning eye, I see." The catgirl's smile widened. "It is good to see there are fans who know this outfit even so far south! I commend you on your— wait a minute!" The catgirl stopped and suddenly pointed a finger at Silva and Kuro. "C-Christopher Redford! Who are these two catgirls?!"

Chris ran a hand through his hair as he turned to Silva and Kuro. "You two, please meet Elsa Redford." Then he turned to Elsa. "Elsa, these two are Kuro and Silva. I believe I mentioned them to you in the email I sent."

"N-Nya ha ha ha! O-of course you did!" Elsa stuttered, her cheeks alight. "I was just so excited to see you again that I forgot half of what you had written!"

Chris deadpanned. "You didn't even read most of my email, did you?"

"Nya ha ha ha ha!"

Of course, Elsa's response was to laugh.

***

Since Chris had introduced Elsa to Silva and Kuro, they quickly hopped on a bus and made their way back to his apartment. Chris carried Elsa's trunk. Since he had mentioned he needed help and that it might take a few days, Elsa had brought a large trunk filled with various toiletries and clothes. She had also, as requested, brought her laptop.

"So this is where you live," Elsa murmured after slipping off her boots. She walked further into the apartment and looked around at everything, nodding approvingly. "It's nice and clean, though it lacks a lot of the decorations I'd normally expect from you."

"Since this is just a temporary place to live, I never bothered decorating," Chris admitted with a shrug. "Anyway, make yourself at home."

"Nya ha ha. Don't mind if I do."

With a grin on her face, Silva bounded across the living room and leapt onto the couch. She bounced once, twice, and then settled down. Still wearing her wide grin, she turned to look at Chris, Kuro, and Silva, who were much slower at getting their shoes off and walking inside. Chris also set Elsa's suitcase against the wall.

"It's warmer in here, but I'm still cold," Kuro muttered bitterly.

"I'll turn on the fire."

Chris wandered over to where his universal remote sat on the coffee table, turned on the fireplace built into his TV stand, and set it back down. Kuro rushed over to the fireplace and sat in front of it, leaving him and Silva to sit on the couch with Elsa.

"Now then, I believe it is time you tell me what you have summoned me for." Elsa crossed her arms and grinned. "I am curious to know what dire situation you have found yourself in. Nya ha ha!"

With that as his initiator, Chris launched into an explanation of everything that had happened up to this point. Of course, by "everything," he meant everything in relationship to Sister Ann, the catgirls living there, the loan she had one month to pay off, and how they planned to solve it. He said nothing about Silva and what she was doing here.

"I understand the situation now. You were right to call me. This is definitely something I can help you with." As she spoke, a broad grin spread across Elsa's face.

"Of that, I have no doubt." Chris returned her smile with one of his own.

"I do have some questions for you, but I suppose those can wait for later. You are pressed for time, correct?" Elsa cracked her knuckles. "In that case, we should get started right now. I'm assuming you want me to set up the Go-Fund Me page? Shall I also set up a Twitter profile for this? I could set up a Facebook page too, but considering the timely nature, Twitter would be better."

"Yes to all the above please," Chris said.

"In that case, I had better get started."

Having said those words, Elsa stood up and wandered over to her suitcase, which she pulled into the living room. She set it on its side. There was a basic security lock on the side, which required an access code to unlock. Elsa tapped several keys, which beeped a number of times, before a soft clicking noise, the sound of locks being undone, echoed around the room.

What lay inside Elsa's suitcase were all the things Chris had expected. Clothes were folded neatly, taking up most of the space, but there was also a bag that contained her toothbrush, toothpaste, and her cat brush. Stashed away in a small pocket at the top was her laptop, which she brought out and set on the coffee table.

The laptop was hot pink. Several stickers of magical wands covered it. There was also, of all things, the image of a teenage boy dressed in a magical girl outfit and embarrassingly covering his crotch.

"I'll be working in the bedroom," Chris said with a gesture. "My computer isn't really meant to be moved. Let me know if any of you need anything."

"I could use some coffee," Elsa said.

"I can make you coffee," Silva said as she stood up.

"Nya ha ha! You have my thanks!"

Since it looked like everything was going well here and Elsa had no complaints, Chris went into his bedroom and started up his computer. He opened CS Photoshop, the program he always used when creating artwork. He'd tried other programs before like Corel Painter, Clip Studio Paint, and Artweaver, but Photoshop was the program he felt most comfortable using.

In the brightly lit bedroom, Chris cracked his knuckles and got to work.

***

Silva did not use a coffee maker to create coffee. Chris didn't have one of those in either event. Coffee makers were large and took up space, and in a kitchen with limited space, such conveniences were discarded.

What she used was a coffee dripper, bright red and made of plastic. She heated water in a steel tea kettle, placed the coffee dripper on top of a large mug, and inserted a coffee filter into the dripper. While waiting for the kettle to whistle, she pulled a canister of ground coffee beans from the fridge. It was the simple Folgers kind, a French Roast. She placed two scoops inside of the dripper. The kettle began whistling, so she took it off, then poured the water into the filter to saturate the ground coffee.

She didn't add all the water at first. She wanted the coffee to bloom. As she waited, the strong scent of ground coffee beans filled her nose and it turned bubbly. It was ready. She poured in the rest of the water, moving in a circle instead of just outright pouring it in. She poured a bit of water in at a time, let it drain, then poured the rest in. After that it was done. She added two scoops of sugar and a small bit of milk.

After placing the filter in the trash and the drip in the sink, she made her way into the living room, where Elsa was hard at work and Kuro was... still sitting by the fire. By this point, the woman had slouched over with her hands held up to the fireplace. Silva shook her head as she set the mug down next to the laptop.

"Here you go," she said.

"Thanks."

Elsa did not do her "nya ha ha ha!" laugh as she continued to work. There was a look of complete concentration etched on her face. She stared at her screen and typed away, fingers flying across the keyboard.

Silva had never seen a Go-Fund Me page before, but she understood enough about the internet to get the gist of what Elsa was doing. At the moment, she was typing information onto the page. It looked like she was setting their goals, the title of their campaign, who they were raising money for, and all the other necessary information.

"There are a few things I'll need before I can complete this," Elsa said with a sigh.

"What do you need?" asked Silva.

"First, we should get a photo of everyone involved with the creation of this page like you, me, and Chris," Elsa began listing off the things she needed. "Second, we should also get a photo of the people at the orphanage. Third, I need information regarding the orphanage, the people living there, and why the people we're trying to convince to give us money should care about why they are giving us money. A sob story is good for PA."

"P... A?"

Silva didn't understand and tilted her head, but Kuro stood up and walked toward them. She sat down next to Elsa and looked at the Go-Fund Me page. While she seemed just as lost as Silva did, it looked like she at least understood something about PA... whatever that was.

"That being the case, tell me a bit more about the people living at this orphanage," Elsa exclaimed. "Leave nothing out. Tell me everything you can. The sadder and more likely to make someone cry it is, the better."

Kuro wore a vicious grin after Elsa said this, which caused SIlva to shudder.

"Everything, you say?"

"Yes. Everything."

And so Kuro told Elsa everything. She told her about how the catgirls she lived with at the orphanage had been physically, mentally, and sexually abused by a man named Markus Flint, how the children there were all abandoned by their parents, and how a loan shark named Calvin Lafaard had tricked Sister Ann into signing a contract for a loan with interest rates so high no one would have ever signed it if they weren't completely desperate. She left nothing out.

By the time she was done, Elsa was a crying wreck.

"Nyaaaa! T-that's so sad!" Large tears streamed from the catgirls eyes and snot ran down her nose. "That is... hic... that's the saddest thing I've ever heard! How could so many bad things possibly happen to such good people!"

Kuro shrugged, even as her lips twisted into a vicious grin. "You wanted a sad story, right? Well, nothing is sadder than the truth."

***

Because she needed pictures of the orphanage for the Go-Fund Me page, Chris, Silva, Kuro, and Elsa decided to travel to the orphanage, which took a good bit of time as they hopped on the bus.

While they were on the bus, a few problems occurred. The biggest one was seating arrangements. Buses weren't small, but they only had two chairs per lane. Chris, Silva, Kuro, and Elsa sat near the back, where two pairs of chairs faced each other, meaning they could at least sit somewhat together.

Silva sat next to Chris.

"N-nya ha ha ha ha! It seems you were quite fast to claim that spot!" Elsa said to Silva, striking an odd pose that Chris was certain he'd seen in at least several anime. "But be prepared! I won't lose next time!"

"Lose... what?" Silva asked, her cutely furrowed brow tempting Chris to lean over and kiss it.

Elsa just responded with her "Nya ha ha ha ha!" laugh.

The bus ride took a long time. Sister Ann's orphanage was on the other side of Chula Vista, which meant it took anywhere from 45 minutes to an hour to reach, depending on factors like traffic and how many stops they had in between. This time it took around 50 minutes. It was already noon when they arrived. Chris glanced up at the midday sun, which warmed his face and caused him to wish he could remain like that for awhile, but duty called.

They traveled to the orphanage and informed Sister Ann of what they wanted. Chris didn't talk to her in her office, which he had Kuro discreetly enter to scout for potential listening devices. She came back about fifteen minutes later and gave him a look. He interpreted it as her wanting to speak with him later.

"I think that's a wonderful idea!" Sister Ann clapped her hands together, her face brightening to the point where Chris thought he might become blinded by her radiance. "Just let me get the kids all together so we can take photos."

"We'll wait outside then," Chris said to her. "Kuro, can you also get the catgirls?"

"Leave it to me," Kuro said as she walked off.

It took longer than Chris would have liked to gather all the children. Some of the kids were all over the place, running around, hiding, and just causing a ruckus. By contrast, the catgirls arrived mere minutes after Kuro went to fetch them.

"Okay, everyone! Smile for the camera!"

Elsa was the photographer, holding her smartphone up in a camera mode that she used to take pictures. It was called the Huawei Mate 20 Pro. Generally speaking, cameras in smartphones had a fairly decent quality, not enough for an amateur to take professional looking photos, but good enough that they were crisp and clean. However, Elsa's phone featured three rear cameras with 40MP, 20MP, and 8MP resolution with a 24MP front-facing shooter and artificial intelligent to help capture great shots. It still didn't make professional photos unless you were a professional, but it definitely helped.

Chris assumed her phone was brand new. His parents must have bought it for her. That reminded him, she didn't have a phone last time, so she must not have had his number. He should give it to her after this.

Photos were taken of all the kids, Sister Ann, and the catgirls. Elsa had them take group photos, individual photos, photos of them in their natural habitat as they played, and everything in between. What Chris originally believed would take only fifteen minutes ended up taking about an hour, maybe even two.

"Your new catgirl is an oddball," a voice said to Chris, causing him to turn.

The person standing beside him was Jason. He smelled of fresh soap and shampoo, so Chris assumed he'd just gotten out of the shower. He was wearing ragged jeans, a white T-shirt, and a black jacket. As always, he looked like quite the delinquent. Chris was reminded of an old movie he watched with his parents once starring John Travolta. What was it called? *Oil*?

"She's actually been with my family since I was a child," Chris corrected.

"Whatever. New to me." Jason rolled his eyes.

"Not gonna get in any of the photos?" asked Chris.

"Do I look photogenic to you?" Jason scowled at him, and Chris had to concede his point with a shrug. As the man watched Elsa go "Nya ha ha!" as she took picture after picture, his expression softened. Chris realized he was looking at Sister Ann. "I don't need to bring any trouble to Annah."

There were any number of things he could have meant with that statement, but Chris assumed he meant trouble would come if a picture of him was taken and it somehow got around. That did make Chris wonder about Jason's background. Was he perhaps hiding some dark past behind that delinquent demeanor of his? Chris didn't know, but it wasn't his place to ask about it, so he kept his mouth shut.

Having focused mostly on his schooling, Chris didn't know too much about Chula Vista's crime rate, but he did know there were a few gangs and that it had a crime index of 38, meaning it was below the halfway point. That was fairly high. So even though he didn't know the number of crimes, if any of those crimes were related to gang violence, or anything else, he knew it was better to err on the side of caution.

Once Elsa was satisfied she had enough pictures, the four of them left the orphanage. They didn't go home. It was late afternoon and Chris was too hungry to take a 45-60 minute bus ride to eat. After walking around for awhile, they found a place to eat.

It was a Korean restaurant located inside of a small strip situated between two residential areas. The mouth-watering scent unique to Korean cooking wafted through the air as they walked in. He could smell grilled meat and soup coming from the kitchen in the back.

This establishment had obviously done its best to present what he believed was a traditional Korean atmosphere. Lintel posts with rope wrapped around the bottom to about a third of the way up went into the ceiling. Several areas were sectioned off by wooden walls that Chris remembered seeing in Asian martial arts films. He glanced at the red walls. There were frames hanging from them. Inside of the frames were Korean symbols. Chris couldn't read them, but he didn't need to.

They ordered their food and then sat at a black square table near the window. Their seating arrangement was a little odd. Elsa was sitting next to Chris, while Silva sat across from him and Kuro across from Elsa. He had expected Silva to sit next to him.

As they took their seats, a young woman in an apron came up and placed water at their table. She was Asian, though Chris couldn't tell what her nationality was from just a glance. Dark eyes, dark hair, and pale skin were her most outstanding features.

"We'll have your order up in just a minute," she said with a smile. No accent. Chris guessed that meant she was born and raised in the US.

As the woman left, Kuro turned to Elsa, her dark eyes boring into the other woman with curiosity.

"Do you think you have enough photos for that Go-Fund Me thing you're working on?" she asked.

"Nya ha ha! I think so. I took a lot of pictures." Elsa crossed her arms and grinned broadly. "I actually took a lot more than we needed. You generally don't want to bombard a Go-Fund Me page with too many pictures. However, having a lot of options to choose from is a good thing. I can pick and choose which pictures to use, and maybe we can use the other pictures for our social media campaign."

"You seem to know a lot about social media and whatnot," Kuro said.

"Nya ha ha ha! But of course! I've been working part-time for the business Momma works at," she proudly proclaimed, thrusting out her large chest, which bounced in the confines of her bra. "I've always had a knack for using computers and love surfing the internet and doing other things. When we were younger, I actually made Chris's web page for his art commissions and helped him get started. Ever since then, Momma has occasionally asked me to do tasks for her involving social media, so I've been learning a lot."

"Elsa has always been something of an internet guru since she first learned how it works," Chris added.

That was putting it mildly, however. Elsa had an insatiable curiosity toward computers, the internet, and all things related to it. When she first learned about it and how it worked, she began reading books to further her knowledge. Theoretical knowledge turned into practical application, which led to her becoming an amateur web designer. That was when she had built his website. Since then, she had become even more adept at learning the ins and outs of the internet and even got into programming.

"You sound really talented," Silva said with a smile.

"Nya ha ha ha! Of course I am! That is why Chris summoned me, after all!"

Their meal came up seconds later.

Chris had ordered a pork stone pot. It was a rice bowl with spicy stir-fried pork bulgogi with onions, scallions, mushrooms, carrots, zucchini, and fresh shredded cabbage with a side of white rice. It looked delicious. As he breathed in the scent, his stomach rumbled, prompting him to grab a set of chopsticks, snap them in half, and dig in.

The others ate as well.

Kuro had gone with a shrimp fried rice cutlet, Elsa a seafood ramen, and Silva a grilled whole mackerel. Each dish looked good on its own. The scents from all four foods mixed together to create an appetizing atmosphere.

As they ate, Chris stopped and stiffened when something soft ran up his leg. The smooth feel of skin and delicate toes rubbing against him let Chris know exactly what it was. He glanced at Silva. She had scooted close to the table and was smiling at him as she ate. Her foot continued to inch up his shin, rubbing against him.

Chris didn't have a foot fetish. Truth be told, except when he was looking at them as a means of cataloging Silva's reactions in bed, he never bothered paying attention to them before. Feet were just feet, and while Silva's were certainly small and cute, they didn't really do anything for him.

Except at this moment.

Having only touched her feet when he was bandaging them after he found her unconscious, Chris had not realized how soft her soles and toes were. Her small toes had the same softness as her hands. However, they were much smaller and seemed even more delicate as she ran them across his leg, traveling higher up.

His breathing hitched as he bit his lip. Should he stop her? It was clear to him that she had gotten this idea from one of the anime they had watched, probably *The Fruits of Grisaia*, which he remembered had a scene where the red-haired female lead had done something similar to the protagonist.

Whether or not Chris enjoyed what she was doing became an irrelevant issue when he looked out the window. A car was driving by. It was a slightly beat up red truck. Nothing special. However, sitting in the back were several men who wore ballcaps, hoodies, and bandanas covering their face.

What struck Chris, what caused his heart to race with fear, was how each of those people was holding a gun.

And all of those guns were pointed into the window of this establishment.

"GET DOWN!" Chris shouted as he tackled Elsa to the floor. At the same time, Kuro had grabbed Silva and tackled her as well. They were just in time.

At that moment, the sound of gunfire and shattering glass echoed all around them.

chapter 9

Chris covered Elsa with his body as gunshots thundered from outside. Glass shattered and screams echoed all around them. Elsa, buried underneath him, looked stunned as shards of glass rained down from above them, hitting his back but not penetrating his skin.

As the gunshots ceased, Chris looked up to find the truck had driven off, but he didn't get up right away. He looked down at Elsa. The catgirl was shivering as the realization of what happened hit her.

"Are you okay?" he asked.

"I'm... I don't know... what... what just happened?" Her words were all jumbled together, like she couldn't figure out if she wanted to ask a question or say something else.

"I'm not sure, but we need to call the police and let them know what happened."

Chris stood up, grabbed Elsa's hand, and pulled her up as well. He glanced out the now shattered window. The truck was long gone. It didn't look like they would be coming back, so he looked at the other side of the table, where Kuro was helping a shaken Silva also stand up. Both of them looked okay. Kuro had a small cut on her forehead and blood ran down her face, but head wounds always bled a lot. The cut didn't look deep.

The first thing Chris did was call the police and let them know about the shooting. He gave them a brief description of what happened and the address. When he subtly mentioned there were catgirls involved, the police said they were sending someone to his position right now and to sit tight.

After calling the police, he made sure the catgirls in his group were okay. Kuro seemed fine. In fact, she didn't seem all that bothered by what happened. There was a scowl on her face, as if she was annoyed, but about the only thing she was worrying over was Silva. Elsa still seemed shaken, and so did Silva.

"I… I don't really understand what happened," his catpanion confessed. "It all happened so fast."

Chris nodded. It happened in the blink of an eye, the truck pulling up, the gunshots filling the restaurant. If Chris hadn't seen them coming before they came up, he would have been too late to warn the others and respond. The thought sent a shiver down his spine. They had avoided death, but he now realized how easily any one of them could have died. That was an unpleasant thought.

The police arrived about five minutes after the shooting. They weren't the only ones. An ambulance had come with them in case anyone was injured.

It was fortunate that no one had been killed or even shot. The bullets had penetrated the walls, lintel posts, tables, and counter, but everyone was miraculously okay. Kuro was the only one with an injury, and she was getting her head bandaged while Chris, Silva, and Elsa were questioned alongside the store owners.

Neither Silva nor Elsa were in any condition to really talk about what happened, so Chris did his best to explain how the truck had pulled up, stopped, fired their guns, and drove off. The police, a pair of white men in the standard uniforms of the San Diego Police Department, took notes as they questioned him.

"Thank you for answering our questions," one of the officers said when Chris finished. "We know it's hard when something like this happens. I'm actually impressed you're so composed."

Chris didn't know if he was composed so much as numb. What happened still didn't feel real, in a way, like he had dreamed all this up. He was sure the events of today would hit him later. However, for now, his mind had settled into a steady state of absolute numbness.

After Chris was questioned, Kuro was asked some questions next. She corroborated what Chris had told them. The process didn't last long. Once the police finished asking their questions, they were free to leave.

As he sat on the bus, Chris thought back to what had happened, to the shooters. Random shootings like this weren't a rare occurrence. There were quite a few shootings where someone just went somewhere, shot a bunch of people, and either left or killed themselves. However, Chris remembered Calvin Lafaard and his comments about how he hoped Chris wouldn't come to regret this decision.

Call him crazy, but he a feeling today's shooting and Lafaard's attempt at paying him off to not help Sister Ann were related.

***

They arrived home over an hour after the shooting took place. While Chris knew they should have worked on their project, no one felt like doing anything. Not him. Not Elsa. Not Silva or Kuro.

Chris did call Sister Ann to let her know about what happened, though he didn't mention his suspicion that Calvin Lafaard had been involved. She had been suitably shocked and gasped over the phone, asking if they were all right, which he had assured him they were. Everyone was shaken to some degree. However, none of them were badly injured.

The rest of the evening was spent sitting on the couch and watching television. Since Silva was the most shaken, he flipped it onto Chef Ramsay's cooking channel. It was another episode of *Hell's Kitchen*.

As they sat squished on the couch, all four of them, Silva used this opportunity to cuddle up to him. Chris easily accepted her soft, warm body into his embrace. He wrapped an arm around her waist as he leaned back against the seat. Silva used his shoulder as a pillow as she curled her feet underneath her bum.

Elsa saw this and laughed. "N-nya ha ha ha! You two seem awfully close, don't you?! But I won't lose out!"

186 Catgirl Doctor Volume 2

"Why do you sound like you're in a competition with someone?" asked Chris.

"Nya ha ha ha!"

Elsa merely released that odd laugh of hers as she took his other side, snuggling herself against his body. She was warm. Her body ran hotter than Silva's, which caused his left side to feel a lot warmer than his right. What's more, Elsa had something his catpanion didn't.

Boobies.

As Elsa's large breasts pressed against him, Chris found it difficult to think. Her boobs were like a pair of pillows pushing against his body. She hadn't always been this big. In fact, it was only within the last two years that her bust size had increased to what they were now. Before that, she was about as small as Silva. He wondered if it was something in the food, or if maybe her mixed breed heritage was the cause for her increase in breast size.

It almost made him forget she was supposed to be his family.

Oddly enough, Silva didn't seem to care as she spoke to Elsa like they were age old friends.

"Do you watch a lot of cooking shows?"

"Nya ha ha! Not really, no. I'm not into cooking and stuff like that, though I do like to eat. I mostly watch anime and sci-fi movies."

"Chris introduced me to some anime. I don't really understand all of it, but there are some really interesting series out there. You watch mostly magical girl stuff, right?"

"Nya ha ha ha! I'm not surprised you can tell!"

"Your outfit gave it away."

Chris didn't interrupt the two as they spoke, since it looked like they were bonding over this conversation and he was loathe to interrupt that. While they talked, he looked at Kuro. She was sitting at the edge of the couch on Silva's other side. She wasn't looking at the TV, however. She was watching him.

The moment their eyes met, Kuro looked away. Odd. However, he didn't think now was the appropriate time to question her.

When the evening sky began growing dark, Chris and Silva went into the kitchen and whipped up a light meal together. Since they had a late lunch, their dinner this time was a simple salad with salmon and a lemony vinaigrette dressing. While Kuro had complained about how the meal was "too light," she did eat all of her food and seemed mostly content.

They didn't run into any problems until later that night.

It happened when Chris mentioned their sleeping arrangements.

"Nya ha ha ha ha! I believe I heard you wrong, Christopher Redford! Did you say I was sleeping on the floor?"

"Not on the floor." Chris tried not to sigh. "On the futon."

He gestured toward the living room floor, upon which a large futon sat. He'd bought this because there was occasionally group projects some of his classes did that involved having people over and staying up late. Since it was just easier to have them spend the night, he'd bought a futon for people to use instead of having them sleep on the floor.

"But why can't I sleep in your bed? It's not like we haven't done it before," Elsa pressed.

But Chris shook his head. "You can't because Silva is sleeping with me."

His words took Elsa aback. She stumbled and stared at him with a wide-eyed stare, then switched her gaze from him to Silva and back again. Finally, she swallowed.

"You and Silva, er, sleep together?" she asked.

"Well, she is my catpanion," Chris said as if the answer was obvious.

Except it didn't seem that way to Elsa. Her eyes grew even wider and she raised a hand to her chest as if the shock was just too much to handle. She staggered back some more, then had to steady herself against the television stand. Her eyes became misty as she stared at him, but she wiped the wetness away before any tears could fall.

Chris became concerned.

"Nya ha... Nya ha ha... your catpanion. I see. I understand the nature of your relationship now." She shook her head and smiled, but her smile was far more bitter than Chris had ever seen it. Brittle was an apt word to describe her smile. "Well, this is a shocker. Nya ha ha."

"Elsa... are you okay?" asked Chris.

"I'm fine." Elsa waved him off as she stood up and walked past him. "I think... I just need to be alone for awhile."

Chris watched helplessly as Elsa walked toward the entrance, slipped on her boots, and walked out.

Silence descended in the room. Chris looked at the other two catgirls. Silva was biting her lower lip, brow furrowed in concern as she stared at the door. On the other hand, Kuro was eyeing him with a curious look that he couldn't figure out.

"I'm going to talk to Elsa," Silva said at last before hurrying toward the door.

Chris thought about following her. He hesitated, however, as he wondered if his presence would be a help or a hindrance. It seemed like Elsa had left because of him, so maybe he would be better off staying here instead of trying to catch her.

"You're not very knowledgeable about women, are you?" asked Kuro.

The question was sudden enough to be startling. He looked in her direction, a frown on his face. However, he also had enough sense to realize the truth in her words. He wasn't dumb enough to dispute them.

"What man is knowledgeable about women?" asked Chris with a shrug.

"True enough." Kuro smiled as if his answer somehow pleased her. "However, since you don't seem to realize why Elsa is upset. Allow me to explain it to you…"

As Kuro explained why Elsa got upset at him, Chris felt his eyes widened until they were the size of golf balls.

***

Silva didn't know where Elsa had gone to. She walked around the second floor for awhile, but she couldn't find the other catgirl anywhere, so she eventually took the stairs to the first floor. She would have taken the elevator, but truth be told, she didn't like elevators. That feeling of her stomach dropping as the elevator moved wasn't pleasant.

She eventually found Elsa after wandering past the main lobby. There was a small sitting area off to the side in a hallway. It had a couple of benches sitting against the wall and two vending machines, one that sold snacks and one that sold drinks. Elsa was sitting on a bench, her tail limp, ears drooping, and tears in her eyes.

"Um, hello," Silva said suddenly.

Elsa jerked her head up, startled red eyes widening when she spotted Silva. She furiously rubbed away the tears spilling down her cheeks, but she couldn't get rid of the red rims or bloodshot eyes. She still tried to though.

"Nya ha ha! I see you've... found me. I'm sorry for running off like that. I didn't mean to worry you."

"It's okay."

Silva walked over to Elsa and sat down next to her. She didn't speak. She wanted to, but Silva honestly wasn't sure what she could say to this catgirl, especially since she was currently feeling a little guilty. Did that mean she should apologize? Silva just didn't know since she'd never been in this situation before.

Just as Silva opened her mouth to say sorry, though for what she didn't know, Elsa spoke first.

"You know, it's really funny. I've loved Chris for as long as I can remember, for about as long as we've been together." She tilted her head toward the ceiling and leaned back, but her eyes were looking at something that Silva couldn't see. The past maybe? "Chris was the one who found me, abandoned in an alley near his home. He brought me home, fed me, bathed me, and let me wear his clothes. He even convinced his parents to adopt me. For as long as I can remember, he's always looked after me, and I love him for that. I love him so much that it hurts… because he never once saw me as anything other than his adopted little sister."

Listening to Elsa's story caused Silva to remember how she had met Chris. A somewhat amused smile lit her face as she realized how similar their stories were.

"Chris… has a knack for rescuing catgirls, doesn't he?"

"Nya ha ha. That he does." Elsa smiled, but the smile soon left as she sighed. "This is very frustrating. Chris has dated a number of girls in his life, but they never lasted long. I don't think they were okay with a guy who lived with a catgirl like me. Maybe they felt threatened. While it was annoying, I could live with him dating those girls because I knew that no matter how many of them expressed an interest in him, they would always leave. I thought I could be content knowing that I was the one constant in his life."

"And now?" asked Silva.

"I'm… really frustrated," Elsa admitted. "I don't want to be his 'little sister' or just a member of the family. I thought I could be content knowing I was the only women who remained interested in him, but knowing he has a catpanion now, someone who isn't me, has made me realize that I can't just accept this. I don't want to."

"I understand how you feel." Silva nodded. "As someone who also loves Chris, I really understand you."

Elsa wiped the tears from her eyes and smiled at her. "Thanks. It's nice to know you can understand where I'm coming from, though I'm kinda peeved at you for becoming Chris's catpanion without me even knowing."

Silva couldn't imagine how much pain Elsa must have gone through knowing the person she loved for years only saw her as a sister. If she had been in her shoes, what would she have done in this situation? Silva didn't know. Given her meek personality, she probably would have quietly accepted it, or maybe she wouldn't have. Had her circumstances been the same as Elsa's, would she have tried harder to make Chris notice her or not tried at all?

In either event, she knew they needed to do something about this.

"Let's go back to Chris's apartment." Silva stood up and held out her hand. "We'll talk to Chris about this. I think if you make your feelings clear, he'll understand and do something about them. I'm sure you know this, but he really cares for you a lot."

"Yeah, I know." Elsa finally smiled as she reached out, grabbed Silva's hands, and allowed the silver-haired catgirl to pull her up. "When I was younger, I used to get sick a lot because I hadn't been vaccinated. My fevers would all run really high, and I was forced into the EU several times because I needed emergency treatments. After that happened several times, Chris told me he was going to become a catgirl doctor so he could take care of me." Her smile widened. "And that's exactly what he's going to college for now."

"That's right, so let's talk to him about this." Silva kept a firm grip on Elsa's hand as she also smiled. "I just know he'll do something to fix this."

***

Chris was sitting on the couch when Silva and Elsa arrived through the door. He glanced their way, stood up, and walked over. Elsa stood nervously before him, but Silva walked behind her and gave the blonde catgirl a push in his direction. She glanced at Silva, who gave her an encouraging nod, then squared her shoulders and returned her gaze to Chris.

"Elsa, can I talk to you?" asked Chris.

"Nya ha ha! Chris, we need to talk," she said at the same time.

They paused and stared at each other.

"I want to talk about—"

"I wanted to apologize for—"

Again. They spoke at the same time. The pause between them lasted longer this time, then they shared a chuckle.

"We used to do this a lot when we were younger," Chris said.

"Yeah." Elsa's smile was nostalgic. "We did."

Coughing into his hand, Chris said, "Anyway, I think we should talk about what just happened."

"I concur," Elsa said.

Silva finally broke into the conversation, clapping her hands together as she smiled. "Since it looks like this is a private conversation, I'm going to let you two talk alone. Where's Kuro?"

"She left," Chris said. "Said she didn't want to be here for whatever drama happens from this."

Silva nodded. "In that case, I'll be in the bedroom. Come get me when you two are done."

Chris trailed his eyes after the silver-haired catgirl as she walked past him, her cat tail swishing behind her, long locks of scintillating hair flowing like a waterfall down her back. She closed the door to the bedroom behind her. Now it was just him and Elsa.

"Why don't we sit down for this?" Chris suggested.

Elsa agreed. "Sure."

They sat on the couch, though they didn't sit as close as they normally did. There was a distance between them now, which Chris knew was his fault, because he'd been stupid and hadn't realized how she felt about him.

Elsa had always been affectionate, but he had honestly just thought it was because they'd grown up together and she was a catgirl, not because of any other reasons. This was his fault. That meant he needed to be the one who fixed it.

"So, um... Kuro told me... you might have feelings for me?"

He winced. Stupid. Stupid. Stupid. If Chris could have kicked himself, he would have done so in a heartbeat. Way to shove your foot up your own ass, champ. He was really impressing himself with his own stupidity these days.

Despite the idiocy of his comment, Elsa smiled even as a soft blush, a light dusting of pink, spread across her pale cheeks.

"Y-yeah, she has it right." Chris snapped his head toward her, causing the hue of her skin to darken as more blood rushed to her face. "I've always loved you. Ever since we were young, I've been in love with you—and not as a little sister or a member of the family. I love you as a woman loves a man, um... what I mean is, if this was an anime, this would be the part where I ask if you'd be willing to give me a litter of kittens."

As she said the words, her face lit up until it was so bright Chris was certain she'd glow in the dark, but now he had an issue. He didn't know what to do about this. How should he deal with Elsa's feelings. This was different from when he turned down Anastasia, who would have never been able to date a guy like him anyway thanks to a certain catgirl. Elsa was someone he'd grown up with since he was young, whom he had treated like his own sister for the past 11 or 12 years, and who had just admitted their feelings weren't on the same page.

She was a lot more important than Anastasia. He loved her. However...

"You know... I'm not sure if I can love you like that yet," Chris admitted.

The look of pain etched onto Elsa's face caused a sharp pain to fill his chest, like a stake was being driven through it. He held strong, though, because he knew his feelings were nowhere near as bad as hers.

"Nya ha... ha ha! Nya ha ha! Yeah, I figured you would say that," Elsa said, taking a shuddering breath. "I just wanted to... wait." She trailed off and looked at him again, her cute nose wiggling alongside her pink mouth. "Did you say yet?"

Chris nodded. "I've only ever thought of you as a sister this whole time, so changing the way I feel about you isn't going to happen overnight... but I want you to know that I'm going try. It might not happen immediately. However, I want you to be happy, and I want to make you happy. I do love you,

you know. Even if it's not in the capacity you want right now."

Tears gathered in Elsa's eyes as she listened to him speak. She sniffled and wiped at them, then broke out into a smile.

"Gosh, I'm crying a lot today. Nya ha ha! This day has been an incredible series of ups and downs," she said.

A wry grin split his lips. "It has. It honestly threw me for a loop when I was told how you felt about me. I had no idea."

"That's because you're an idiot."

"I wish I could argue against that, but I feel like I don't have any room to stand on right now."

They shared a chuckle before Chris stood up. He stretched his arms, feeling his back pop. A groan escaped from his mouth. As he brought his arms back down, he smiled at Elsa.

"I'm going to get ready for bed. Since Kuro isn't here anymore, would you be okay sleeping on the couch?"

Elsa did not look satisfied with the idea of sleeping on the couch, but she seemed to understand there wasn't much that could be done right now. Sure, he could give her the bed. In fact, that was probably what he should have done but... well, call him clingy, but he wanted to sleep while snuggling with Silva.

Chris was just about to leave for the restroom. He turned around and walked past her, but before he could make it two steps, Elsa grabbed his arm.

"Is something wrong?" he asked, turning to look at her.

"No. I just…" Elsa's cheeks flushed a furious red like the crimson color of fire engine, but she swallowed her nerves and made her request. "Um, we haven't… hugged at all since I arrived. Not even once. We used to hug all the time, so I was wondering if we could now… if you want to, I mean."

Chris only now realized he hadn't hugged Elsa at all like he normally did when they were together. Perhaps he had subconsciously tried to keep his distance because of Silva. He didn't know, but he also understood that wasn't the right way to go about this, no matter whether he could love Elsa as something other than his sister or not.

"Yeah. Sorry about that."

He leaned down and pulled Elsa to him, wrapping his arms around her tiny waist. As she pressed her body against his, her breasts smashed into his chest, and Chris, against his will, stiffened up like a block of ice—a block of ice that was quickly melting as Elsa's warm body rubbed against him.

Elsa giggled. "You say you don't love me, but you are clearly excited to see me."

"I... It's a natural physical reaction." Were the only words the blushing Chris could use to defend himself as he readjusted his pants.

chapter 10

The Advocation of Catgirl Rights Society's Convention was located at the Los Angeles Convention center, a massive hosting facility for all sorts of events. It was made of mostly glass and cement. Many of the walls looked like they were composed entirely of glass. The building was divided into two parts, attached together by a walkway that traveled across the street. The main convention center, which was shaped like a rounded triangle was where the Catgirl Convention was taking place.

Chris was taken aback by how crowded it was. He, Silva, Elsa, Kuro, Sister Ann, the Siamese twins Lin and Lacy, and the tabby cat with boyishly short hair Elizabeth stood before the entrance and watched as hundreds, maybe even thousands of people came and went. It was unbelievable. So many different people had come to this convention. Old people. Young people. Men. Women. Catgirls. There was a group of catgirls dressed in maid costumes handing out fliers for a cafe. There were humans wearing fake ears and tails taking pictures with many catgirls. It was almost like a catgirl paradise.

"I've never seen so many people," Lin muttered.

"Neither have I," Lacy said.

"That's because we've always been together," Lin said.

"Oh. Right."

Chris glanced at the Siamese twins, then looked at Kuro with a raised eyebrow for an explanation.

"They grew up in a small orphanage just outside of San Diego. It's a relatively remote location. I'm not sure how Markus Flint managed to find them," Kuro explained.

"Ah." Chris nodded.

"I'm getting a little nervous," Silva finally muttered as she placed a hand against her chest. Her breathing was heavy. "This is… a lot more people than I'm used to."

Chris and Silva had been traveling outside regularly for quite a while now, but while she could shop at stores and go to the movies, that didn't mean she was used to being around this many people. Chula Vista was a large city, but it was spread out. She'd never had to deal with such a large mass of humanity in a single place. They were like sardines in a can.

Opening his mouth to give her some reassurances, Chris found himself interrupted by the most unlikely of sources.

"Nya ha ha ha ha! Do not worry! You aren't alone, right?!" Decked out in her magical girl cosplay, Elsa dashed in front of the group, spun around, and struck a classic magical girl pose. "All of us are here with you. With the power of friendship, there is nothing we can't face together!"

A moment of silence passed as everyone stared at Elsa, who remained locked in her magical girl pose. They were speechless. Even Chris didn't know exactly what he should say in a situation like this.

Kuro was the first to recover. She summed up all their thoughts quite succinctly.

"That was incredibly cliché."

Everyone else nodded their heads.

"H-how rude!" Elsa shouted.

However, just as she finished shouting at them, an elderly couple came up. Gray hair. Wrinkles along their mouth and eyes. They were just a stereotypical pair of old people, but with them was a young catgirl who couldn't have been older than six or seven. The catgirl, a purebred Birman cat with creamy blonde hair, was staring at Elsa with stars in her eyes.

"Excuse me," the old woman said. "But my granddaughter noticed your costume and absolutely loves it. Can she take a picture with you?"

"Of course!" Elsa said, her anger now forgotten as she and the excited young catgirl struck a pose for the old couples camera.

"She gets distracted easily, doesn't she?" Elizabeth mumbled.

"That's part of Elsa's charm," Chris said with a shrug.

Since standing around wasn't doing them any favors, the large group moved closer to the convention center. As they did, Chris kept turning his head, looking for the familiar blonde hair of the woman they were supposed to meet here. The others also knew they were meeting someone just outside of the convention center, but they didn't know what to look for. He would have shown them a picture, but he sadly had no pictures of Anastasia Pierce.

Fortunately, the person looking for them noticed their presence before they noticed hers.

"Chris! Chris!"

Anastasia waved at them from near the entrance. They all stopped as she trotted toward them.

Perhaps it was due to the event taking place right now, but Anastasia had dolled herself up in skintight black hosiery that was partially translucent, a red jacket that trailed past her waist, and a black skirt/white shirt combo that revealed a hint of her stomach. She was wearing makeup too. It was more than what she usually wore, but not enough that Chris thought it looked gaudy. Ruby lips. A hint of mascara. Some eyeshadow. There was just enough to highlight her most striking features.

"Anastasia, allow me to introduce you to everyone," Chris said in greeting before he introduced her to Kuro, Lin, Lacy, Elizabeth, Sister Ann, Elsa, and finally, Silva.

When he reached Silva, Anastasia turned ridged, though it only lasted for a moment. Yet even after she relaxed, her eyes bored into Silva's. This resulted in the silver-haired catgirl looking away.

"So you are the one who stole Chris away from me," Anastasia said with a chuckle.

"Oh. Um…"

Silva didn't look like she knew how to respond to the human woman's provocation. She dithered in silence, mouth opening and closing. Her actions caused Chris to step forward, preparing to chastise his friend for her actions, but Anastasia just chuckled.

"Relax, I'm only teasing." He didn't think she was teasing, but he knew this was probably the most revenge she'd get over what happened. "Now then, you three are a bit early for your presentation. Fortunately, Mother's panel regarding catgirl rights, which is where she'll allow you to plead your case, isn't for another hour. That said, you are just in time to help at Mother's booth. We have a pair of catgirls who will be going on break soon, so we need some people to replace them."

The catgirls with Chris suddenly gulped when Anastasia looked at them with a somewhat vicious gleam in her eyes. However, none of them could say anything as she led them into the convention.

They were stopped at the front, but Anastasia had come prepared and given each of them a badge so they could get past security. Of course, he called it security, but it was really just a few few guards checking bags and making sure the people coming into the convention center had a pass. Once they were through, the woman continued leading them deeper into the convention center, until they were being directed inside of a large room that looked like a changing room.

"You stay out here," Anastasia said to Chris before slamming the door in his face.

Chris sighed as he leaned against the wall and waited. Several people walked past him. All of them were a mixture of humans and catgirls. There were some catgirls who looked like high school students. They were with their friends, human girls who walked alongside them, giggling about one thing or another. A couple of middle-aged folks were also present, walking through the hall to their next destination. He was surprised by how vastly different in age people attending this convention were.

About twenty minutes after he was told to stay outside, the doors opened. Chris turned around to face the catgirls. His breath was promptly stolen from him.

The girls weren't wearing anything immodest, certainly nothing like the sexy cosplay he'd seen at anime conventions, but the outfits they wore still left him breathless. They were wearing black and white maid uniforms. The white under dress was short-sleeved and had a gap near the front that revealed a small hint of cleavage. A bodice-like dress went over the top, fitting snugly around the waist to emphasize their breasts, and it was followed by a white apron with small, colorful bows on either side. Their outfits were finished by a standard headpiece.

Only Sister Ann and Anastasia were not wearing these outfits, but even the sister wore catgirl ears on her head and had a fake tail sticking out of her backside.

"Wow," Chris muttered. "You girls look amazing."

"Do you... like this style of dress?" asked Silva, seemingly a tad hesitant as she grabbed the hems and swished the ends around.

"I wouldn't say I'm a fan of maid outfits, if that's what you mean," Chris said, then smiled. "But I do think it looks great on you."

Silva beamed brightly at his compliment, but Kuro was scowling as she towered over the others. She was wearing the same outfit as everyone else. This made her look like a super buff maid.

"I don't think I look good in this thing at all," she stated.

"I disagree," Chris said with a shake of his head. "You might think you don't look good in that because you're so much taller and more muscular than everyone else, but I think that makes you look exotic. You're different. If I were to give your outfit a cosplay name, I'd say you look like a military maid or maybe even a mercenary maid."

"A mercenary maid?" Kuro frowned.

Chris nodded. "A badass maid who can kick ass even better than she can serve. To be honest, I think clothes are really attractive on you."

There was just something about a strong and muscular woman in a maid outfit that drew people's attention. Kuro was tall, which automatically meant she was the most visible person in the group, but she also had a commanding presence that made her impossible to ignore. Her muscular arms were on full display, her massive chest was bouncing as she moved, barely constrained by her bra and the white dress, and her long black tail and messy hair gave her a somewhat ferocious look that clashed with the maid outfit. However, it was that very clashing aesthetic that made her appearance so appealing.

"Well…" Kuro looked away and crossed her arms. "I guess that's fine."

"I've never worn something like this before," Lin said.

"Neither have I," admitted Lacy.

"Of course not." Lin rolled her eyes. "You've always worn the same clothing I have."

"I know that," Lacy said with a scowl.

"N-now now, you two," said Elizabeth as she tried to calm the duo down.

"Nya ha ha ha!" Elsa placed her hands on her hips and thrust out her chest. Chris eyed the jiggling jugs bouncing around in his field of vision warily. He hoped she would accidentally smack someone with those. "I'm not usually one for maid outfits, but I suppose I can wear one just this once."

"In any case, now that you girls are dressed, follow me," Anastasia said. "We have a booth in the exhibit hall that you'll need to man for awhile."

"Um… what should I do?" asked Sister Ann.

"Just stick close to me," Anastasia said. "Your part won't take place until my mother's panel."

As the name suggested, the exhibit hall was just a massive space on the first floor that resembled a warehouse. It was filled with thousands of people and hundreds of booths displaying everything from catgirl products to brochures that taught the basics of catgirl physiology. There was even one booth that offered catgirl massages, which had people lay on a table while a tiny Singapoura catgirl stepped on them with her bare feet.

He'd actually heard about that. It was called Ashiatsu, the ancient practice which involves a massage therapist literally walking on someone's back. It had been performed by Buddhist monks for centuries before making its way across the world. "Ashi" meant foot and "atsu" meant pressure. There was supposed to be some kind of chi and zen aspect to this form of massage, but Chris only understood the very basics of it.

The booth Anastasia's mother had them manning was one that offered brochures. These brochures spoke of the process necessary to adopt a catgirl, why adopting a catgirl was a great idea, and how it could help humans and catgirls grow closer. It was a simple guide. Chris read through the brochure Anastasia handed him and found that it spoke in layman's terms, making it easy to understand.

Only a few minutes had passed, but the catgirls he'd come with were already in the process of handing out brochures. He hadn't known why they needed to wear maid outfits at first. Now he knew, however. They were drawing quite the crowd. The tiny but adorable Silva as she blushed and stuttered, the cute twins and their back and forth banter, Kuro and her incredible physique, Elizabeth with her creamy blonde hair and attractive features, and Elsa with her flamboyant personality and beautiful looks. Each catgirl was different, and those differences stood out with those maid outfits, helping further bring attention to them.

He was worried about whether or not Silva would be able to deal with so many people. She had never been good in crowds. However, Elsa and Kuro were sticking right next to the girl, funneling most of the people toward them so Silva only needed to deal with one or two individuals at a time. Seeing this caused warmth to spread through his chest.

"You know, I'm really surprised you've decided to help your mother out here," Chris said at some point.

"Why is that so surprising?" asked Anastasia.

The two of them were behind the booth instead of in front of it. Their job was not to hand out fliers but answer any questions someone might have regarding the information inside of the brochure. However, very few people actually came up to them, more enamored by the catgirls themselves than the information contained inside.

"Because I know you don't really like her," Chris answered with a shrug.

"Just because I don't get along with my mother doesn't mean I dislike her," Anastasia said. "Besides, even if I didn't like her, she is the one paying my tuition. I can't exactly tell her off now, can I?"

"I suppose not."

"You don't get along with your mother?" Sister Ann asked, sounding saddened by that information.

"Not particularly," Anastasia admitted but refused to go into detail.

Chris wasn't sure how much time they spent down in the exhibit hall, but Anastasia eventually received a text message from her mom. She looked at the phone, reading the message, then sighed and turned to Sister Ann.

"It looks like you're up," she said.

"O-oh? Am I... um..."

"You'll be speaking to a crowd of people at the panel my mother is on right now, pleading your case to them and asking for donations. Fortunately, mother has already received the Power Point presentation Chris made, so the only thing you'll have to do is talk while everyone watches the presentation," Anastasia said.

"I-I see." Sister Ann still looked nervous about speaking in front of a large crowd of people, but she took a deep breath and tried to harden herself. "Please lead the way."

"Right." Anastasia turned to Chris. "I'd like you to remain here with the catgirls and man the booth."

"I can do that," Chris assured her with a smile.

Anastasia smiled back. "You know, I've been thinking about this for awhile now… and I think it's a good thing you didn't accept my feelings back then. A relationship between you and me would have never worked out."

Chris tilted his head, not understanding why she was telling him this now, but Anastasia's smile just widened as she lead Sister Ann away from the booth and out of the exhibit hall.

***

Chris had no idea what took place during the panel. He had stayed in the exhibition hall with the catgirls. He and the catgirls were relieved of duty about two hours after they started, so they had all wandered around the exhibit hall and looked at the many different booths.

Silva had remained plastered to his side. It seemed like, after dealing with so many people for so long, she had reached her limit. She hugged his arm close as they walked. However, she didn't shiver or appear frightened by being around so many people, just exhausted. He was honestly quite proud of her, and he made sure to tell her so by whispering in her ear.

While Silva remained with him and Kuro stayed by Silva's side, the other catgirls were being led by the rambunctious Elsa, who had seamlessly inserted herself into the group with her bright and bubbly personality. She seemed to get along particularly well with the twins. However, Chris did have to put a stop to her antics when she began teaching them magical girl poses.

A lot of people came up to their group and asked for pictures. The catgirls were still wearing their maid uniforms, so he guessed everyone assumed they were part of a maid cafe or maybe cosplayers. There were a lot of people, humans and catgirls, who were dressed in costumes, though none of them were anywhere near as exotic as the cosplay found at places like the San Diego Comic Con or Anime Expo.

About one hour after being relieved of duty, Chris received a text message from Anastasia telling him the panel was done and they should meet her and Sister Ann outside.

Finding them wasn't easy. Maybe it was the late hour, but it seemed like there were even more people outside now than there had been when they first arrived. Large food trucks sat on the roadside, selling all kinds of delicious food, the scent of which caused Kuro's and Elsa's stomachs to rumble.

"Nya ha ha! Chris, I want something to eat please. Can we get some food?" Elsa asked, whirling on him.

Chris thought about it for a moment, calculating how much money he could afford to spend in his head. On top of doing the work for this convention, he'd also done a lot of commissions, so he had a little more money than usual. He believed he could afford the overly expensive food truck prices.

"Sure, let's all grab something to eat," Chris said.

"Yes!" Elsa leapt up and pumped her fists into the air. Chris shook his head when he saw how her large chest bounced around despite being confined by a bra.

There were four food trucks in total. All of them were manned by a human and catgirl pair. One of them sold crepes filled with everything from meat and vegetables to fruit and whipped cream, while another sold Indian food like curry and kebabs. There was another that sold Mediterranean food and the last one sold standard American cuisine like hotdogs and hamburgers.

All the catgirls unanimously chose to get crepes, and they chose the sweetest crepes available. He was almost positive the reason for that was the whipped cream. Every catgirl released a content "meow" as they licked at the whipped cream within the crepes while they sat down on a bench next to a cement garden with several trees.

As they sat there, Anastasia and Sister Ann finally emerged from the convention center. The sister looked exhausted. There were bags under her eyes and her shoulders were slouched as the two shambled over to his group. However, she also wore a satisfied smile.

"How did it go?" asked Chris as he stood up.

"I think it went well," Sister Ann said.

"She did a very good job despite being a nervous wreck," Anastasia added. "I'm certain quite a few of the people who were present for the panel will donate to her Go-Fund Me page now. We're actually so late in getting out because a lot of people came up to express their concern for her plight and encouraged her not to lose hope."

"I'm glad to hear that," Chris said. "So does that mean we're done here?"

"It does," Anastasia said.

"In that case, I think we're going to take our leave." Chris glanced at the catgirls. Most of them had finished their meals and were now leaning against each other as they slept. Silva was leaning on Kuro, the twins were leaning against Elsa, and Elizabeth had curled up on the bench to take a catnap. All of them had worked harder than he was sure they ever had.

"That's probably a good idea," Anastasia admitted.

"Thanks again for helping us," Chris said with a smile, but Anastasia waved him off.

***

A few days passed since the convention. Chris still had four more days before he could go back to school. During his time at home, Anastasia had emailed him a recording of all Professor Shinomiya's lectures alongside the notes she had taken in class, which made it incredibly easy to record everything in his notebook.

Silva and Elsa had played together while he worked on his schoolwork and commissions. They would watch TV, go outside (though they didn't leave Memorial Park), and play video games (Elsa got Silva into them), which he thought was a good thing. It was great to see them getting along.

Chris still wasn't sure what he should do about Elsa. He knew their relationship would eventually have to change. Nothing can remain the same forever, but he really did need time to overcome the large hurdle that were his own emotions. Chris didn't want to take that next step in their relationship until he was sure he could see her as a woman and not the adopted little sister he'd lived with for several years.

Kuro hadn't come over since the convention, but he was certain the catgirl was busy helping out at the orphanage. He didn't know what was happening yet since he hadn't taken a look at their Go-Fund Me page. After the convention, he'd handed over the administration rights to Sister Ann.

It was Friday evening. Elsa and Silva were playing a game called God Eater for the PSP. It was a Japanese action RPG developed by Namco Bandai. Chris had read an article once about how it was Bandai's answer to Capcom's Monster Hunter series, an incredibly popular franchise that Chris had played. He even had the latest version for his Xbox One.

Chris was using Elsa's laptop to get some work done, since it allowed him to stay in the living room with the two catgirls, who were currently sitting next to each other on the couch as they played. He only had one PSP, the one Silva was using, but Elsa had her own. He hadn't even realized she'd brought it along until she whipped it out one night and demanded Silva play with her.

Chris sat at the table, the laptop in front of him as he typed into it. He'd just finished all of his work and decided to finally take a look at the Go-Fund Me page Elsa had created for Sister Ann. As he brought up the Go-Fund Me homepage for their fundraiser, he blinked in surprise.

The top of the page featured a large image of Sister Ann surrounded by the children of the orphanage and the catgirls who live there. It was a heartwarming image, but it was also heartrending. The children were all smiling and happy.

Meanwhile, the background showed the dilapidated orphanage. While it wasn't the main focus of the photo, which was the kids, just having it in the background was enough to show how poor they were.

That wasn't what caught his attention, however.

It was the number on the screen.

"Two hundred and fifty thousand…"

The original goal of this fundraiser was to raise $125,000 so Sister Ann could pay off Calvin Lafaard. They had reached and exceeded that goal by a large margin, doubling the amount of money she needed to pay off her debt.

Of course, Chris acknowledged that he hadn't done much. He made the artwork, the banner, and helped Elsa create the PowerPoint presentation, but everything else had been done by Sister Ann and the others.

He shut off the laptop, closed it, and was just about to head over to the couch, when the clicking of his lock reached his ears. Chris turned toward the door just in time to see Kuro throwing the door open and marching inside. She was carrying a paper bag and wearing the widest grin he'd ever seen on her. He couldn't remember a single time they had met where she looked so happy.

"We did it!" Kuro cheered. "Did you see the numbers?! The Go-Fund Me has barely even been up for a week and we've already made twice as much as we're supposed to!"

"I saw," Chris said as he stood up.

Meanwhile, Silva and Elsa stopped playing their video game. Elsa, dressed not in her magical girl outfit but a pair of yellow pajamas that matched her hair, grinned as she leapt to her feet. She wasn't wearing a bra right now, so her large chest jiggled more than usual inside her shirt. Chris needed to look away from her, lest he become distracted.

"Nya ha ha ha! Of course we did!" she exclaimed as Silva slowly stood up and smiled at Kuro. "Did you expect anything less to happen when Chris and I got involved? Nya ha ha ha ha!"

"Thank you!"

"Nya ha—urk!"

Chris winced when Kuro lifted Elsa into a ferocious bear hug. He didn't think the bigger catgirl meant to, but her hug was so strong that Elsa released a pained croak, and Chris could have sworn he heard the magical girl wannabe's back cracking. Kuro didn't seem to notice, however. She swung the now limp catgirl back and forth. Chris watched as the poor Elsa's limp legs swung around like noodles before shaking his head.

After dropping the nearly unconscious Elsa onto the couch, Kuro grinned as she grabbed the bag she'd dropped and held it up with a grin.

"I brought catnip and alcohol to celebrate," she said excitedly.

What followed was a mini-celebration as Chris sipped at the alcohol Kuro had brought, a kind of Japanese whiskey called Suntory Toki, and watched as Silva and Elsa got completely high on catnip.

"Nya ha ha ha ha ha ha! You look so funny! I just wanna rub your cheeks!"

"Hnn... I feel really hot. W-why is my body so warm? Uwu, I need to get out of my clothes."

It had been funny watching Elsa rub her cheek against Silva's as she hugged the other catgirl to her lap, but once Silva began stripping, Chris had to put his foot down. He was all for her getting naked. However, he didn't want to deal with the raging hard on he would have while Kuro and Elsa were present. It would have been problematic.

The two catgirls eventually passed out. Elsa ended up lying on the floor, on her back, with her feet and hands sticking in the air. Her mouth was wide open in a dopey smile as she drooled. Meanwhile, Silva had fallen asleep with her head on Chris's lap. Her body was curled up on the couch. As he sat there and stroked her hair, Kuro was sipping a glass of whiskey as she sat beside them and watched Silva with what appeared to be envy.

"I noticed you haven't had any of the catnip you brought," Chris said at last.

"I'm actually not fond of the stuff," Kuro said with a wan smile. "When I was in the military, someone tried to dope me up on catnip because he thought that would make it easier to have his way with me. While I showed him I was no easy target, it still made my fondness for the stuff disappear."

Chris nodded but didn't inquire into what happened further. He wasn't sure how important it was for him to know this, and it wasn't like knowing made a difference anyway. It was just something that had happened in the past.

"I want to thank you," Kuro said at last. "You really helped us out. I'm not sure what we would have done if Sister Ann's orphanage had closed."

"I'm sure the government would have helped you relocate to another orphanage or even let you stay in their catgirl only housing units," Chris said.

"Maybe, but that would have meant separating us." Kuro took another sip of her glass. "Part of the reason we decided to stay with Sister Ann was because none of us wanted to be separated. During our time as prisoners, we all grew very close. Silva is a newbie, so she isn't as close to the other catgirls as I am, but some of us have known each other for over a year."

Her cheeks were turning pink from the alcohol. Chris glanced at the bottle and realized it was half empty, but he'd only had one glass, so she must have drank the rest. No wonder she was being so open. That much alcohol would loosen anyone's lips.

"I understand not wanting to be separated after going through what you did—well, not really, but I understand the idea." Chris turned thoughtful. "It would be hard bonding with others who haven't shared your experiences."

"Exactly." Kuro nodded.

They elapsed into silence for several minutes, but Chris eventually decided he should put Silva to bed. He lifted the girl into a princess carry, traveled into his bedroom, and tucked the girl into bed. Reaching out, he brushed the bangs away from Silva's face. She looked so cute and innocent that he couldn't help but press a kiss to her forehead.

However, just as Chris was about to get into bed, Kuro appeared in the bedroom.

"Kuro?" Chris asked when he saw her. "What's up?"

"There's something else I wanted to talk to you about," Kuro said as she walked up to him, and something in her walk, which reminded him of a jungle predator stalking its prey, made his spine tingle.

"What is it?" asked Chris.

He wasn't sure what she wanted, but whatever it was, he didn't expect the woman march over and press her lips to his. She was much taller than him, about a head taller. Kuro had to lean down to kiss him, but once she pressed their lips together, her tongue was filling his mouth, stirring up saliva and sending new sensations rocking through his body.

"K-Kuro," Chris gasped as he pulled back, "w-we can't do this!"

"Why not?" Kuro asked with a frown.

"Why not?" Chris gawked. "Because Silva is my—"

"I don't mind."

A voice came from the bed, causing Chris to turn his head and discover that Silva was wide awake and watching them with bright eyes. The soft smile on her face took Chris's breath away. However, her words left him stunned.

"You don't?"

Silva shook her head. "I knew Kuro had feelings for you for awhile now, though she was having trouble admitting it. I told her that she should think it over, and if she decided to become your catpanion, she shouldn't hold herself back."

Chris was stunned. Unlike Elsa, who Chris had mistaken her love for sisterly affection, Kuro hadn't really given him any indication that she loved him or even found him attractive —barring that one incident at Tanner's kickboxing center. However, it wasn't like a single embarrassing incident was enough to make someone love another. He and Kuro had spent a lot of time together, but nothing romantic had ever really happened between them.

"Is that... how you really feel?" Chris asked.

Kuro nodded. "It is. I've been watching you this whole time. You're hard-working, compassionate, and helpful. You go out of your way to help others. What's more, you're strong and you have a rocking body." She grinned. "For your information, I'm really fond of men with nice muscles. I was attracted to you the moment I saw you exercising at the kickboxing center."

"I had no idea," Chris admitted.

"I don't make my feelings as obvious as Silva and Elsa do." Kuro shrugged. "I wouldn't expect you to know how I feel without me telling you." She paused. "Now that you know this, what are you going to do?"

Chris understood what she meant. She was asking if he would accept her as his second catpanion, if he would accept her feelings and return them, or not accept her feelings and turn her down. While part of him was uncertain about accepting this woman, he also couldn't deny there was a much larger part that was happy to accept her feelings.

"Are you sure I'm good enough for you?" asked Chris.

"Would I be willing to become your catpanion if I wasn't?" Kuro shot back.

"Good point." Chris accepted those words with a nod. "If that's how you feel, and if Silva really is okay with it, then I have no reason to not accept you. I really respect you, and I won't deny that I think you're gorgeous." He suddenly grinned. "For your information, while I find women like Silva unbearably attractive and cute, I also find tall women with muscles attractive too."

Kuro matched his grin. "I know. You're the kind of guy who can find just about any body type attractive."

"That's… true enough, I guess."

Chris scratched the back of his neck, but he didn't have time for anything else as Kuro leaned down and began kissing him again. It was a little different because he had to tilt his head to kiss her. He was used to kissing women smaller than he was. However, the idea of such a tall woman passionately pushing her tongue into his mouth as she smashed her massive tits to his body was enough to turn his loins into an inferno.

At some point during their kiss, Silva had climbed off the bed and got behind Chris. She unbuttoned his flannel shirt and slid it down his arms, tossing it aside before pressing her chest into his back. She must have taken her shirt off. Her stiff nipples poked against him. A feeling like lightning raced through those nipples and into his body. Those feelings only became more accentuated as Silva began nibbling on his ears and licking his neck.

At the same time, Kuro had placed her hands on his chest and stomach, feeling them up as though she was creating a topographical map of his body. Her hands were large. They weren't the dainty hands most catgirls had. They were rough and calloused from serving in the military, which might have been the reason he was reminded of a jungle cat like a jaguar instead of a housecat.

As the kiss continued, Kuro lifted Chris off his feet and tossed him onto the bed. He squawked in surprise as he flew through the air and landed with a bounce.

"W-what was that for?!"

Kuro grinned as she and Silva climbed onto the bed and grabbed his pajama pants.

"What do you mean? We can't take the next logical step if we aren't on the bed," Kuro said.

"But did you have to throw me?" Chris asked.

"Yes."

With that simple answer, Kuro removed his pajamas and boxers in a single go, then stared at his dick as it sprang free. Her eyes widened.

"I knew it was big from when I pinned you down during our spar several days ago, but I hadn't realized it would be so massive." Chris felt his chest swell with stupid male pride. He knew it was dumb, but having a woman call his dick massive gave him a huge ego boost. "How the fuck did this monster fit in Silva's tiny little cunt?"

Chris blinked at the sudden expletives spewing from Kuro's mouth. He would have wondered if they were the results of her drinking too much or something else, but he would never get the chance to ask about it.

Because Silva and Kuro began licking his cock.

"Hrg!"

Chris nearly swallowed his tongue as the two leaned over and took their tongues to his dick. Kuro trailed her tongue from his balls all the way to his head. Meanwhile, Silva was licking the sides, completely naked, her small breasts barely visible between her hair. She was moaning and mewling as she licked him. Chris realized only after several seconds had passed that the reason was because she was masturbating while licking his cock like a popsicle. One of her hands was cupping her vagina, and he could see the beginning of her love juices trickling down her thighs.

It didn't take long before he felt his balls tighten.

"Y-you two! If you keep doing that, I'm gonna—"

At those words, Kuro gently pushed Silva away and leaned down. Chris's eyes widened as his dick was engulfed in the warm and wet cavity that was her mouth. She didn't just stop with taking him in, however, as she went down all the way until her nose was pressed against his crotch. He could actually feel his dick going down her throat. When combined with the way her rough tongue rubbed against his shaft, Chris was unable to even consider holding himself back.

He exploded inside of her.

It was probably because his dick was literally pressing into her throat, but her cheeks didn't bulge and nothing leaked out of her mouth as he shot his seed inside of her.

With a grin, Kuro slowly removed his dick from her mouth. She trailed her tongue along the underside of his cock as she released him with a loud plop. The electric sensation that shot through his dick made it semi-hard once more, and Kuro smiled when she saw that.

She climbed off the bed and began removing her clothes, first lifting her white sleeveless muscle shirt over her head and tossing it to the floor. Then she removed her white bra, which created an incredible contrast with her dark complexion. As the bra was removed, her massive breasts sprang free with a jiggle, dark brown nipples visibly stiff. The way they pressed together as they hung on her ribcage was impressive. Had he ever seen someone with such large tits? No, he concluded. No, he hadn't. Even Elsa was a little smaller than her.

"Do you like my breasts?" asked Kuro.

"They might be the most magnificent breasts I've ever seen," he admitted.

"Then… what about my breasts?" asked a pouting Silva as she reached out her hands and cupped her small chest.

Chris smiled. "Your breasts fit you perfectly, and I love their size and shape, so please don't pout—actually, you know what? You look even more adorable when you pout. Please keep pouting."

While Silva's cheeks swelled like someone had shoved balloons into them, Kuro laughed loudly as she removed her pants, socks, and panties. Now stark naked, she climbed back onto the bed and straddled his legs. Her thighs were every bit as muscular and magnificent as her arms. However, what really drew Chris's attention and made his mouth go dry was her stomach. He'd seen some women with a six-pack before, but never had he seen one that was so well-defined, so incredibly tight and perfect. Her washboard abs would have put all the men and women he knew to shame.

"Now, it's time for me to claim this cock as my own," Kuro said as she rocked her hips forward. Her pussy came into contact with his dick, and she ground it against him. The feeling of her warm nether lips and soft patch of trim pubic hair rubbing his cock made it grow stiff once again despite having already cum.

Silva pouted some more. "That isn't your cock to claim."

Kuro smiled. "Don't worry. I know he was yours first. I'm not going to steal him from you, especially since you were kind enough to share him with me. This is our cock."

"That's better," Silva said with a nod.

"I've noticed that you're only this resolute about matters when it involves sex," Chris said to Silva.

"I don't know what you mean by that."

Before he would respond with a witty retort, Kuro had grabbed his shaft and guided it into her entrance. She didn't even hesitate to shove her hips down, engulfing his dick in a single go. She wasn't tight like Silva. However, the ridges of her vagina felt a lot different, which meant this was a unique experience. The soft warmth of her insides conformed to his shape and rubbed against him in all sorts of amazing ways. As she placed her hands on his chest, lifted her hips, and slammed it back down, sensations like bolts of lightning traveled from his cock and straight to his brain. He tried to thrust his hips, but Kuro used her weight and superior strength to keep him from moving.

"Nu-uh," she said with a grin that showed her sharp canines. "You're not supposed to move. I'm the one in charge here."

Chris was unable to do or say anything as she began thrusting her hips again, increasing her pace, decreasing her pace, grinding against him. She constantly changed things up, leaving him unable to so much as say a word. All he could do was grunt and groan. Unlike Silva, who had only experienced sex the one time Markus raped her, Kuro obviously had a lot of experience, and she was using it to thoroughly dominate him.

He found that he didn't mind. Actually, this was turning him on so much it cast a white haze over his mind.

As Chris was drowning in pleasure, lying on the bed, a shadow appeared over him. He blinked when he found a dripping wet snatch right in front of his face. The glistening lips of Silva's outer labia was something he'd recognize even while lost in the throes of pleasure. Her pussy was puffy with arousal. Her clit looked like it was bulging slightly, perhaps because of how furiously she had been pleasuring herself.

"Chris... meow to... I want to be pleasured to... S'il vous plaît..."

Did she just speak French?

Chris was too lost in the experience of Kuro driving him to delirium to do anything more than obey Silva's request. He leaned forward and buried his nose in her ass and his tongue in her pussy. He lapped at the juices already dripping down her thighs and pussy, spreading apart her vagina to reach her tight little passage.

"Mreow!"

As he fucked her with his tongue, Silva ground her mound against his face. Her loud, ragged gasps mixed with the moans and grunts from Kuro, whose actions still caused electricity and fire to race through his dick. He could already feel his balls swelling up again, feel the pressure building in his abs, and knew he was close.

Chris didn't want to be the only one who came. He reached his arms around Silva's legs and rubbed her clit between his fingers. Between his tongue action and his fingers, Silva's entire body became taught. Her thighs enclosed around his head and shook as she arched her back, until her head was pressed against the headboard and she was releasing a loud "MREOW!" that echoed along the ceiling. As her juices flooded over his face, Chris felt his own release as white hot pleasure raced through his body.

And then it was over.

Chris lay on the bed, gasping for breath as Silva snuggled into his side. Kuro was lying next to him, her chest jiggling with every heaving breath she took. He glanced at her, at those massive tits and that perfect six-pack, and he felt his dick twitch, though it didn't get back up. He was too exhausted.

"That was… incredible," he gasped.

"Wasn't it?" Kuro said with a gleam in her eyes. "I haven't had this much fun with a man in a long, long, long time."

"H-how long is a long, long, long time?" he asked, curious.

"Hmm…" Kuro looked thoughtful as she reached down and slowly stroked her engorged pussy. The sight caused him to gulp. "Probably about… six years or so. Very few men can make me cum like you did. Markus certainly couldn't get me off, the fucker. He only ever cared about his own pleasure to begin with, but even if he had been a great man I was willing to have sex with, his pecker had been so tiny I could barely feel it when he penetrated me."

Chris could not believe Kuro could so easily talk about what happened to her, but he also understood she wasn't Silva, who was fragile and became easily emotional. Kuro was a warrior, a fighter, and a motherly figure to the other catgirls. She was also the strongest person he knew, both physically and mentally.

"Well," he huffed as his heart rate slowed down, "I'm glad I could please you."

Kuro chuckled. "Me too."

They lay in silence for a time.

"So… catpanion?" Chris asked.

"That's right." Kuro nodded. "I am now your catpanion, but don't expect me to be like Silva over there." She gestured toward the content and utterly blissed out catgirl sleeping on his other side. "I'm not the kind of cat who will just let you do whatever you want. If you want something from me, you've got to take it, because you can be damn sure I'll take you whenever I want."

Chris laughed. "F-fair enough. I'll remember that."

"You had better." Kuro grinned as she rolled onto her side, scooted close, and grabbed both him and Silva. "Now be a good body pillow and snuggle with me."

As the large, muscular woman wrapped a leg and arm over his and Silva's bodies, Chris realized he might have bitten off a little more than he could chew with this woman, who could so thoroughly dominate him it wasn't even funny.

Oddly enough, he didn't mind.

Those were his thoughts as he closed his eyes and went to sleep.

To Be Continued...

Afterward

Hello, everyone! I hope you all enjoyed Catgirl Doctor 2. I must admit, while I enjoy writing stories that have a heavy plot line, complex characters, and an epic journey filled with action and adventure, sometimes I just want to write hentai.

Speaking of, if you enjoyed Catgirl Doctor 2, please consider writing a review. Books live and die by their reviews. If you'd like to see this book and future books in this series thrive, writing a review is the best way to help it continue living. That said, my greatest hope is that you enjoyed the story.

Catgirl Doctor 2 is when I finally introduce Chris's harem. For those who are wondering, Silva, Elsa, and Kuro are the only members of Chris's harem and I won't be adding anymore. While this series is very much an erotic story about a dude having vanilla sex with his harem of cute catgirls, I dislike large harems because it becomes harder to keep track of all the characters and give each one their own unique personality and motivation. Some authors are great at writing stories with big harems. I am not.

Outside of the harem dynamics and relationship building, the one thing this story has is a surprisingly dark plot. The first volume was about Silva, a rape victim, and her journey to heal with Chris's help. This volume not only introduces several new characters, but expands upon the plot thread of Silva's capture and assault by introducing Calvin. I don't want to say too much about him because spoilers. What I can say is that Chris has found himself in a much larger scheme than he could have ever realized when he first discovered Silva.

Before I head off, I would like to give thanks to a few people.

I first want to thank my artist. Liremi has been going through some personal problems that I won't get into. Suffice to say, this year has been a little rough for her, which is why I am very grateful she was willing to continue working with me. Her artwork is some of the best I've seen.

I also want to thank my copy editor and proofreaders for helping me fix up my grammar. I can't say this story is perfect, but they do a great job fixing up many of the bigger issues my writing has.

Lastly, I want to thank all of you for reading this story. I'm a little worried Catgirl Doctor won't be as popular as my other stories because of it's nature. That's why I'm incredibly grateful to everyone who read and enjoyed it. I hope you will all join me again when volume 3 comes out.

~Brandon Varnell

Like manga? Brandon is adapting his American Kitsune light novel series into a manga on Patreon!

HAVE YOU EVER EXPERIENCED ONE OF THOSE LIFE-CHANGING INSTANCES? AN EVENT SO MOMENTOUS THAT, YEARS LATER, YOU'RE STILL MARVELING AT HOW IT CHANGED YOUR LIFE?

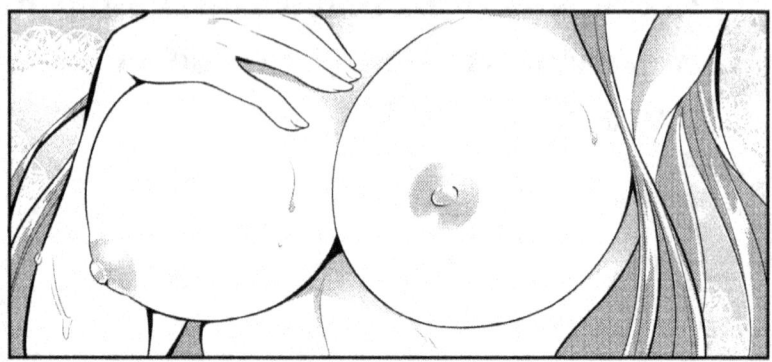

I HAD ONE OF THOSE. IT HAPPENED A WHILE AGO

EVEN TO THIS DAY, THROUGH ALL THE CHANGES THAT HAVE HAPPENED, THROUGH ALL THE EXPERIENCES THAT I'VE BEEN THROUGH, I STILL CAN'T BELIEVE HOW THIS ONE MOMENT CHANGED MY LIFE FOREVER.

NO MATTER WHAT CAME AFTER, OUR FIRST MEETING IS SOMETHING THAT I'LL ALWAYS REMEMBER.

ESPECIALLY SINCE, AT THE BEGINNING OF THIS TALE, I THOUGHT SHE WAS NOTHING BUT AN ORDINARY FOX WITH, UNORDINARILY ENOUGH, TWO BUSHY RED TAILS.

LIFE

.

.

.

.

.

.

.

.

.

.

IT HITS YOU WHEN YOU LEAST EXPECT IT TO.

Hey, did you know?
Brandon Varnell has started a Patreon
You can get all kinds of awesome exclusives
Like:

1. The chance to read his stories before anyone else!
2. Free ebooks!
3. exclusive SFW and NSFW artwork!
4. Signed paperback copies!
Er... maybe we don't want that last one, but the rest is pretty cool, right?

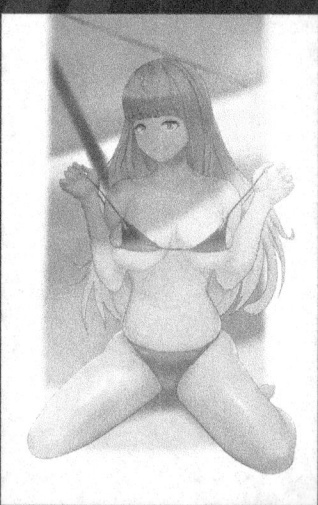

To get this awesome exlusive conent go to:
https://www.patreon.com/BrandonVarnell
and sigh up today!

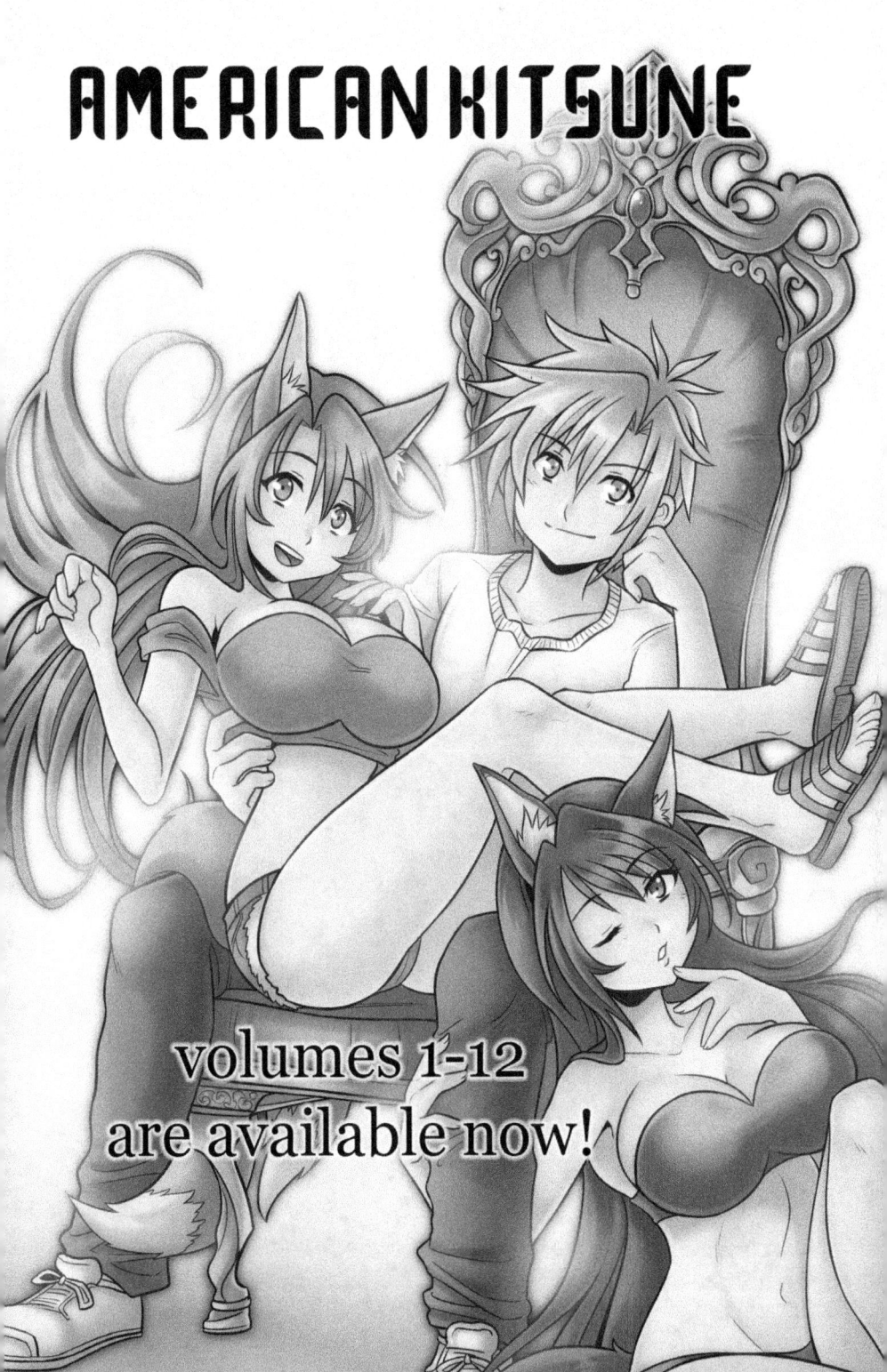

AMERICAN KITSUNE

volumes 1-12
are available now!

Available in
paperback, kindle,
and Kindle Unlimited!

A
Most
Unlikely
Hero

Available in paperback, kindle,
and kindle unlimited!
WIEDERGEBURT
LEGEND OF THE REINCARNATED WARRIOR

MMG-001
NOW AVAILABLE ON
PAPERBACK, KINDLE, AND
KINDLE UNLIMITED!
MAN
MADE
GOD

INCUBUS

VERTICAL

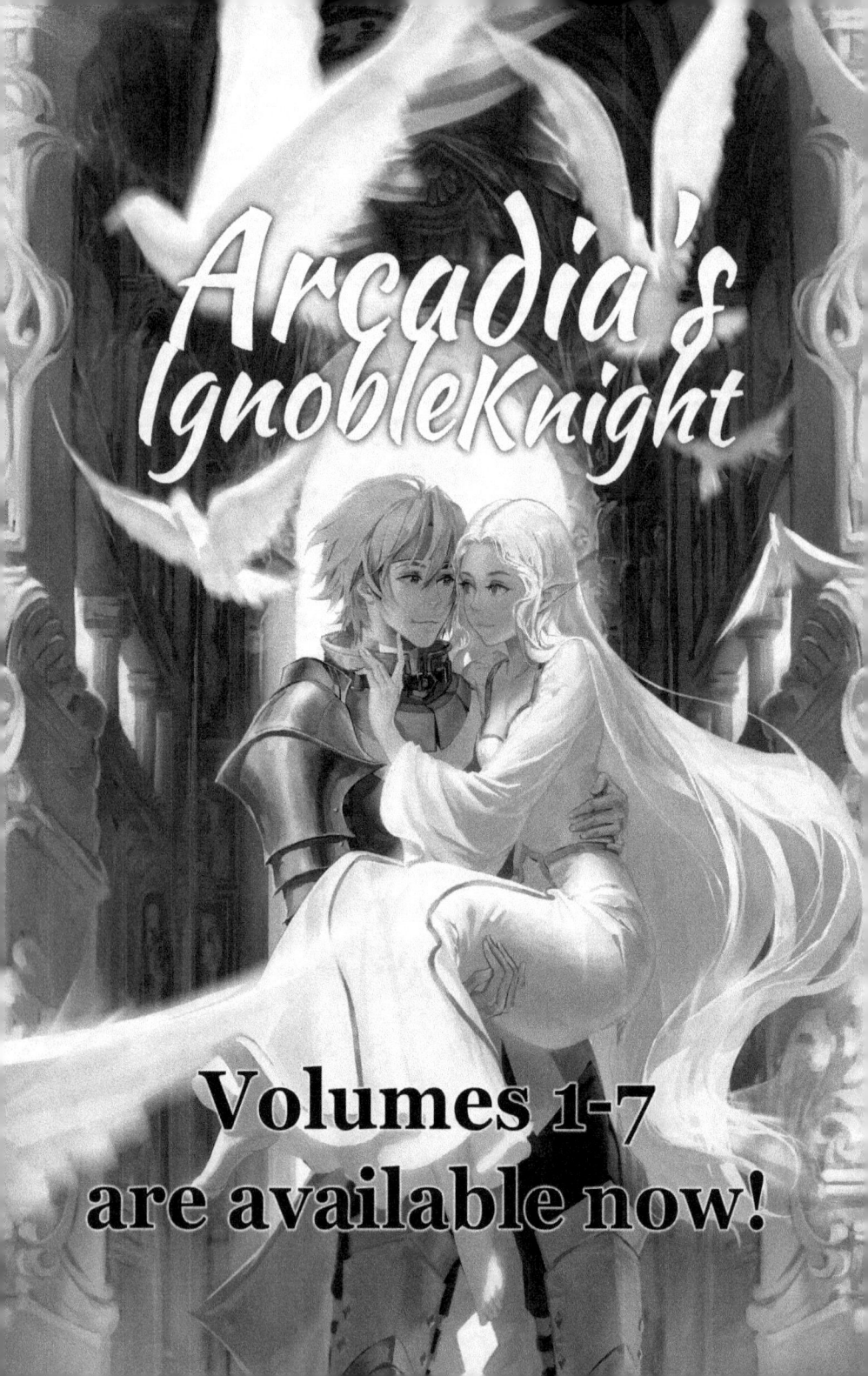

Arcadia's IgnobleKnight

Volumes 1-7
are available now!

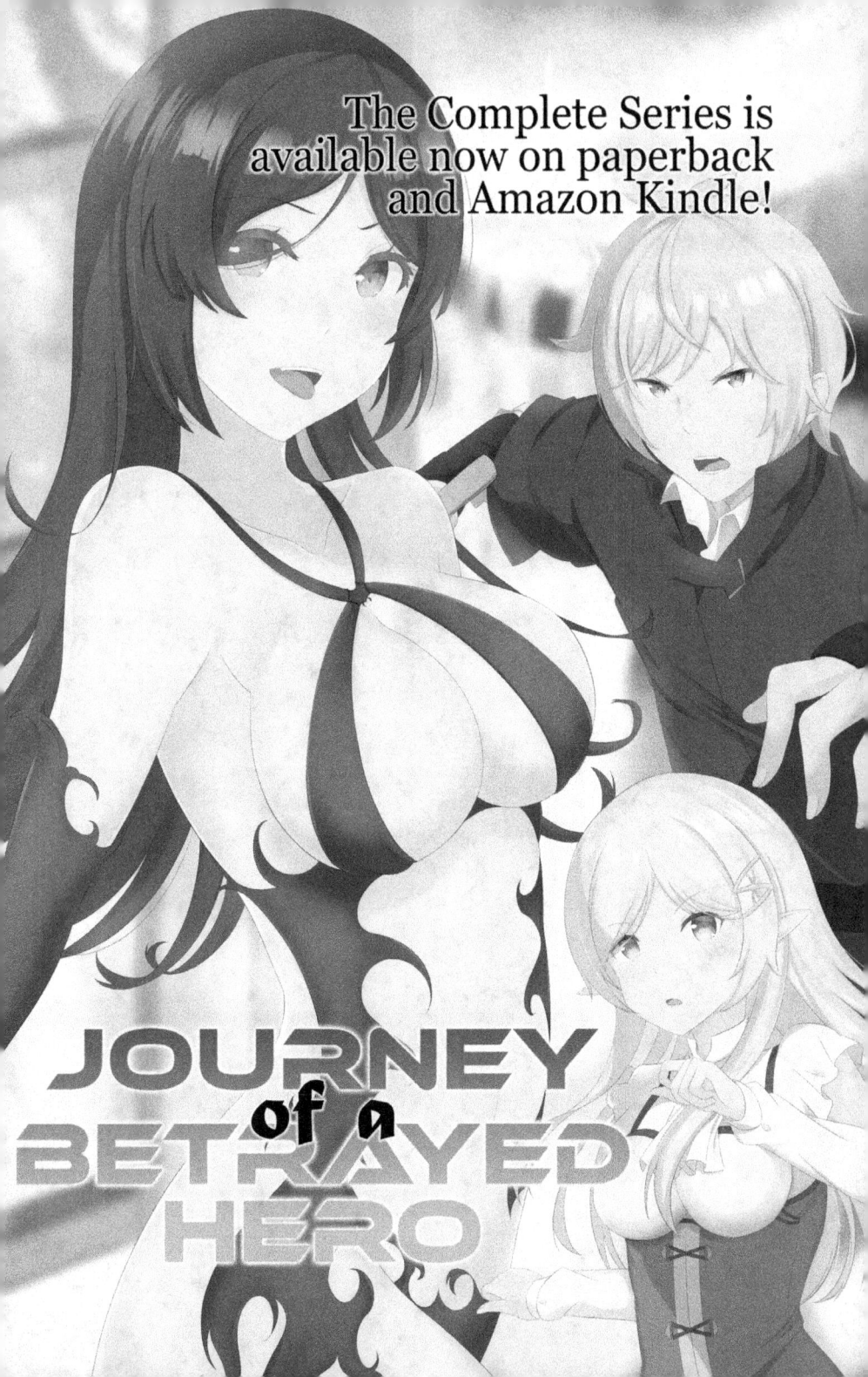

JOURNEY of a BETRAYED HERO

Volumes 1 & 2 are available on
paperback,
Amazon,
and Kindle Unlimited

Swordsman Of the Rift 2

Want to learn when a new book comes out?
Follow me on Social Media!

 @AmericanKitsune

 +BrandonVarnell

 @BrandonBVarnell

 http://bvarnell1101.tumblr.com/

 Brandon Varnell

 BrandonbVarnell

 https://www.patreon.com/
BrandonVarnell